THE DISCOVERY MACHINE

Thomas Clinton Procter

THE DISCOVERY MACHINE

© 2009 Thomas Clinton Procter

ISBN: 978-1-61170-049-7

This is a book of fiction. The characters, names, incidents, organizations, and dialogue in this novel are either products of the author's imagination or are used fictitiously.

Cover design by Joleen Guzman
Chapter illustrations by Ariel Lacey

Printed in the USA and UK on acid-free paper

For additional copies of this book go to:
www.rp-author.com/procter

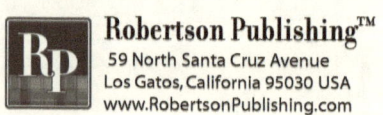
Robertson Publishing™
59 North Santa Cruz Avenue
Los Gatos, California 95030 USA
www.RobertsonPublishing.com

We have all heard of Young America. He is the most current youth of the age. Some think him conceited, and arrogant; but has he not reason to entertain a rather extensive opinion of himself? Is he not the inventor and owner of the present, and sole hope for the future?

Abraham Lincoln
February 11, 1859
Jacksonville, Illinois

DEDICATION

This book is dedicated to Elena Thomas and her son Randy McMullin, whose unwavering examples of a lifetime dedication to doing the right thing in life, with love, was behind the motivation and support for this writing.

OTHER ACKNOWLEDGEMENTS

My heartfelt thanks to my friends Brian and Cathy Plowman, whose belief in this project and unselfish help, made the project possible. Also, special thanks to Madison A. Miller, who at age thirteen provided me with realistic peer insight in the form of her special editing of the text. And thanks to my friends at Acura in Santa Clara, California.

TABLE OF CONTENTS

PREFACE

The small northern California village of Los Gatos is slow-stirring at 7:00 a.m. It's like something out of a storybook, quiet and picturesque, and filled with classic Americana shops and interesting places. The town is nestled on the edge of a small range of mountains some twenty miles inland from the ocean at Santa Cruz, traversed across a winding and sometimes dangerous Highway 17. A good part of Los Gatos is divided by a stream leading away from a large dam and lake about two miles above. The south edge of the village falls gradually away into the valley, which holds the tenth largest city in the United States, San Jose.

The Silicon Valley lies nearby, and is a major influence in all that happens in this vast and diverse area of population and business that stretches from Los Gatos in the south to San Francisco in the north. The influence of the technology-based center of the United States permeates the everyday life of all that live and play here, especially the children. Already a fertile environment for anyone of creative leanings, it is said that there is almost a magical air that exists for those children who wish to push their imagination, and pursue dreams beyond normal comprehension. The schools in the area employ teachers who are aware of this formative environment, and intelligently encourage their students to explore their dreams, and venture into pursuits not yet traveled.

It is in this atmosphere of creativity that two very inquisitive ninth graders from Los Gatos High School set forth on an incredible adventure that changed not only their lives, but those of their family, friends, and even the world in which they continue to explore.

Now, open your minds to your inner imagination, however dormant it may be, shed as many of the experiences you may have that might stand in the way of your freedom of mental exploration and experimentation, and let yourself completely go. If you do, you will be surprised at what happens.

It *may* just change *your* life.

CHAPTER ONE: FIRST VENTURE

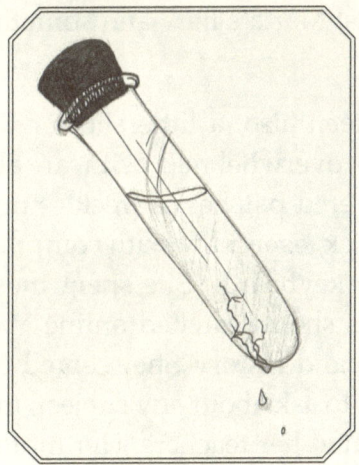

That morning started not unlike any other morning. The light breeze that nudged the window blinds slightly gave no whisper of what was to happen, and even the light clustering of clouds in the almost flawless blue-skied panorama above gave no hint of what lay ahead. At least for two 9th graders.

It was Saturday morning, and Phillip and Maria were lying face down on the floor with their heads on their hands, looking at pictures in magazines, and perusing encyclopedias. They were best of friends, and had been so since their earliest memories of kindergarten. Teachers over the years had consistently remarked at how the two children had become inseparable. Their intense friendship had only intensified as they grew older, and was enhanced by the fact that their homes were only two blocks apart.

At thirteen, Phillip was slightly taller but more slender than his 9th grade classmates. He had intense blue eyes that peered curiously through his wire-framed glasses at the world around him. The lenses hid partially beneath thick shafts of wavy brown hair, which he was constantly brushing from his eyes. He was very sharp, and already knew more about computers and programming than most experienced adults, as well as having a good grasp of elementary physics. He just seemed to have an inherent feel for machines, and was good at visualizing concepts and designing them. He was also very calm by nature, which was a good balance against Maria's fiery and sometimes quick to anger personality.

Maria was thirteen also, a little shorter than Phillip, with a uniquely cute face overwhelmed with an abundance of curly red hair, which covered patches of freckles on both cheeks. Like Phillip, she was quick, especially with computers, and was faster than Phillip on the keyboard. She spent most of her time concentrating on topics she researched online about her two favorite subjects, science and history. She seemed to know by instinct just what questions to ask about any subject, most of which either delighted or frustrated her teachers. Her mother, a widow of ten years, was a very private woman, but intensely proud of Maria's intelligence. She always chose her words carefully when speaking of her daughter, and would quietly describe her as "inquisitive".

Maria and Phillip were unique for 9th graders, and functioned on a level of maturity more like Seniors in High School, both in conversation and action. Their other schoolmates just didn't understand a friendship of that type. They were annoyed by what they interpreted as aloofness from the pair, and called them stuck up. They made fun of them, and teased them a lot about being nerdy. As a result, Phillip and Maria tended to keep pretty much to themselves. They enjoyed that anyway, as the bond they had created over the years tended to create activities that mostly excluded others, if for no other reason than a practical one of time and interest. And Maria had zero patience for anyone with what she called "an attitude." They enjoyed their time together, and were sometimes a little selfish about it.

Phillip and Maria were on the floor together, when the moment actually arrived. Maria looked up from her encyclopedia, studied the paper clip she had been using to mark where she was in the book, looked at Phillip briefly, and then from out of nowhere, she said, "Phillip."

Phillip dragged his eyes away from the page and looked up.

"Phillip, look at this." She handed him the paper clip.

Phillip took the clip between his fingers and studied it closely. He looked curiously at Maria. "What about it? Am I missing something?"

"Yes, Phillip. You are. Me too. I think we all are. All the time. I mean, just what do you see? Take a good look at it. What do you think about that paper clip?"

Phillip paused and looked into Maria's eyes. Then he looked back down at the clip, stood up slowly, and went over to his desk where he sat down and put the clip under his desk lamp. He bent over it and turned it over and over in his hands, feeling its texture, studying it. He moved it from one hand to the other as if feeling its weight. He pulled the clip lightly testing the strength of the bent curves. He held it up to the light. He finally swiveled around in his chair and peered at Maria over the top of his glasses.

"O.K. Red," he said. He was used to Maria testing him for reactions. "Let's see. This particular clip is about two and a half inches long, and it appears to be made of steel or at least some hardened alloy." He paused and looked at Maria for some sign of encouragement. Seeing no reaction, he continued. "We use this for holding things together, like papers. It is a pretty common item, and I guess we would call it a tool. Everyone has these in their desks and drawers. It's actually a pretty cool invention."

Maria's eyes lit up. "Exactly! That's exactly it! It *is* a cool invention. It is basic and simple and we all use it every day. But you know what? I would bet that very few people ever think about how it came to be invented. Or *who* invented it. We just take it for granted that it is here."

3

She pursed her lips, shrugged her shoulders, thought quietly for a moment, then suddenly jumped up. "Oh, Phillip! Wouldn't it be fun if we could travel to the moment in time when an inventor actually came up with the idea for an invention, and watch how he discovered and put it together?"

Phillip took a breath, thinking as he took in what Maria had said. Then his eyes began to widen behind his glasses.

"Maria." He turned to her and said quietly, "*That* is a great concept. I love it. But you are talking about time travel."

"Yep," Maria said smiling. "I'm aware of that. It's just a concept." She smiled again. "But wouldn't it be great to be able to do it? Think of the fun it would be."

Phillip and Maria studied each other quietly. Phillip looked out the window for a few moments. He turned back to Maria.

"I love this concept, Maria," he said. "I absolutely love it. And, uh, well, I, I, uh . . I..."-

Maria laughed. "What's up? Are you going to weird out on me now?"

"Well," he began hesitantly, "coincidentally, I have just discovered something weird, and have been thinking about a machine for months . . ." He paused and drifted into his thoughts for a moment. "Hmmmmn." He peered at Maria over the top of his glasses, and studied her for a few more moments. "I'll tell you what. Give me about a month and I'll show you what I've come up with. O.K.?"

Maria could hardly contain her excitement. "I'll hold you to it," she said. "I'll wait for your call on this, but I'm warning you, I'm not going to be patient." She moved to the door. "In the meantime, I have to go home. I'll see you at school."

And with that, Maria left, and Phillip went into his workroom and sat down at his desk. He picked up a pencil and his sketch pad.

The next few weeks Phillip and Maria didn't see each other very much, except for classes they shared at school. Maria bugged him constantly about what he was doing with the project. He would just smile, and say, "Patience."

After school hours were filled with Phillip working late into the night in his workshop, making many trips out of the house to return later laden down with boxes, and more boxes, which he trundled laboriously upstairs to his workroom. His mother and father, used to his eccentric projects, seldom saw Phillip at dinner time, catching only blurs of him whirring past the dinner table, grabbing handfuls of food on a plate which he balanced going up the stairs. They even heard him late at night after they had gone to bed, making heavy dragging sounds like furniture going up the stairs. "Just leave him be," Maryanne would say to her husband. "He's o.k., and we need to encourage his creativity."

Three weeks later, on a sunny Saturday, he called Maria on the phone, and whispered excitedly into the receiver, "Maria, the prototype is done! Please come over!"

When Maria arrived, Phillip took her hand and led her into his workroom upstairs. Maria was very familiar with the workroom and Phillip's environment at home. She knew by heart each item hanging on the walls, each piece of laboratory equipment, and each diagram they had sketched in their many projects together.

Phillip closed the door behind him and turned on the lights. Before them stood a large object covered by a blanket.

Maria looked at Phillip. He smiled. "Go ahead," he said. "Pull the cover off."

Maria grabbed the blanket edge with both hands and pulled it off quickly. She gasped.

"I call it the Discovery Machine."

She stepped back in amazement. Before them stood a strange object almost six feet high. It sat on a round base of metal, wood, and plastic, and was covered with gears, wheels, levers, several small video screens that looked suspiciously like some small T.V. sets found formerly elsewhere in his house, and a keyboard suspended below some dials. Two easy chairs covered in red velvet cloth sat in the inside of the contraption, and a two foot wide panel with several gauges was fastened above the keyboard about head-high. Two large push-buttons were at arm's reach in front of the chairs, and they had been marked in bright blue letters that read, "TRAVEL", and "RETURN".

"Those chairs, "she said pointing at the two large easy chairs. "How in the world did you — "

"It wasn't easy," Phillip said with a grimace.

"Is it safe?" Maria asked, a little nervous about the idea of traveling to another time. "If this works and we actually go somewhere, are you sure we will get back o.k.?"

"Of course!" Phillip said, with his fingers crossed and hidden behind his back. "Where do we want to go first?" he added quickly.

"You mean *now?* You want to go somewhere at this moment? Just like that?"

"Yup. Just like that."

"Well!" was all Maria could find to say. She stood there with her hands on her hips. She was trying to be brave, but she was having doubts about jumping into this.

They sat down on the floor together and thought. They looked at pictures. They talked quietly.

After a long time, Phillip sat up quickly and said, "Well, I guess anything would work just to try this out. Right? Then, how about Silly Putty? Have you ever wondered how that stuff ever came about?"

Maria looked a little perplexed.

"Well," Phillip said with a smile, "I was curious about it a while back, and I at least know when and where it was invented."

They looked at each other. Maria shrugged her shoulders with a "why not" expression, and walked nervously over to the Machine. Phillip jumped up and extended his hand down for her.

"Let's do it. Let's go find out!" They buckled themselves in.

Phillip said, "Ready?"

Maria nodded, now speechless.

Phillip reached forward, typed the words, "Silly Putty" on the keyboard, placed his hands on the "TRAVEL" button, looked at a very wide-eyed Maria, and when she nodded, pushed the button.

The gears in the machine began to whir, and the platform started vibrating softly. They felt themselves moving out through the walls of the house, as if they weren't there, first slowly, then rapidly increasing in speed. The scene around the machine began to blur, going in and out of focus. Then they caught glimpses of scenery speeding around them, and it felt like the machine was caught in a huge wind of some type that was sucking them into some dark abyss.

After what seemed like an eternity, the whirring and blurring began to slow down, and the scenes around the machine began to come more into focus.

With their hearts beating wildly, Phillip and Maria found themselves gliding softly to rest on the ground, in an area in the back of what appeared to be a parking lot, surrounded by trees.

It was a beautiful morning in the summer of 1943, according to the screen on the machine, and the screen briefly described that the large building beside them was a laboratory in New Haven, Connecticut, owned by General Electric.

Still in shock and very shaky about their incredible first trip on the Discovery Machine, they eased carefully down from the machine and sat on the ground leaning against it. They took long, deep breaths, trying to calm the pounding of their hearts from what they had just gone through.

After a while, Maria said, "O.K. Mr. Inventor, what do we do now?"

Phillip smiled, breathing easier. "Well, I do know that the inventor's name was James Wright, and he was working for General Electric on a contract for the Government trying to come up with some sort of substitute for synthetic rubber. It was in the middle of World War II, and I guess the government was trying to come up with all sorts of substitute products for materials used in the war time effort. I also found out that even though Mr. Wright made the discovery, it was another man later who made it famous by marketing it." He smiled. "But we can talk about that later."

He pointed at the large official looking building alongside the parking lot. "I would assume that is the laboratory where he is working." He scratched his head thoughtfully. "I'm not sure how we will find him, or watch Silly Putty being discovered."

They sat there for a while, and finally Maria smiled and said, "Why don't we just simply go to the reception desk and tell them we are on a school project to interview Mr. Wright? It might be just simple enough to work. What do you think?"

Phillip pursed his lips. He stood up abruptly, and helped Maria to her feet. "Let's go try it. What do we have to lose?"

They went around to the front of the building, walked through the main doors, spotted the reception desk, and walked over to it. There was a large, stern-looking man sitting behind a circular desk studying some papers in his hand. He was wearing an impressive blue uniform with a shiny badge on his chest. He looked up as the children approached.

"Well," he said with just a hint of a smile on his face, setting his papers down, "What can I do for you two young folks?" He looked them over carefully.

8

Maria had her most sincere and pure expression on her face, one that she knew would get the most respect from adults.

"Well, Sir, we are on an important school project. We would like to interview Mr. James Wright, because we know he is an important scientist, and uh, and we just wonder if we might talk to him for a few moments." She put on her most imploring look. "Could we please?"

The man looked at Maria intently for a moment, then Phillip. It seemed like an eternity. Phillip was smiling sincerely, but holding his breath.

"You say this is a school project?"

"Yes," Maria said, nodding her head. "It's very important. If we get an interview with Mr. Wright and turn in a good report, we could get an "A!" And not only that," she added enthusiastically, "We might be able to get places in a new science program at school."

"Well," the man said slowly, smiling. "Well," he said again. "Pursuing a science career is definitely admirable." He tapped his fingers slowly on the desk top, and then paused. "If I were able to get you an interview with Mr. Wright, would you promise to send me a copy of that report?"

"Oh yes! Yes! We promise!" Maria said, glancing sideways at Phillip. Phillip's smile was frozen on his face as if painted there.

The man smiled. "Well, I happen to know that Mr. Wright is just about to go on his lunch break." He picked up the desk phone and dialed a number. "Let's just see if he could take some time for you."

He turned his attention to the phone. "Oh, hello, Mr. Wright. Ah, Mr. Wright, I know this is a strange question, but I have two young budding scientists here," he glanced at Maria and Phillip again, "I'd say about twelve or thirteen years old, who tell me they are on an important mission from their school to interview you personally. Yes. Yes. That's what they said. Yes, I think so." The man laughed. "No, I don't think they are a security threat. Yes, I think so too." He laughed again as he listened to what the man on the other end of the line was saying. "You can spare them some time right now? Fine, Mr. Wright. I'll send them right up." He hung up the phone and stood up.

"You are two very lucky kids. Mr. Wright said that if you go up right now, he'll grant you a few minutes for an interview. Is that O.K.?"

"That's great!" Maria gushed. "How do we get up there?"

"Well," the man said, "Because of the security we have here, I will have to walk you up there." He pushed a key on the board in front of him, and picked up two tags with long neck chains. The tags read, "Visitor". He handed one to each of them. "Put these on." He picked up his keys and an official-looking clipboard. "Just follow me."

As they fell in behind the guard, putting their tags on, Phillip leaned over and whispered in Maria's ear, "*That* was amazing. You can really lay it on thick!"

Maria elbowed him affectionately. "I know." She laughed.

They followed the guard up an escalator to the second floor, then down a long corridor, and stopped in front of two large doors. There was a phone to the right of the doors. The guard picked up the phone and dialed, and then set the phone back in its cradle as a buzzer sounded. He pulled the door open and they walked inside.

They entered a large room filled with exceptionally long tables, and cabinets loaded with strange looking equipment. Microscopes of all sizes were everywhere, along with large photo machines, x-ray machines, sinks and water equipment apparatus. Open cabinets revealed all sorts of chemicals and solvents, and several machines that appeared to be ovens of some type were placed throughout the room.

Smaller rooms with what appeared to be very specialized strange-looking equipment branched off from the main room, and from one of those rooms a slender man with white hair and glasses emerged and walked toward them. He was dressed in a white laboratory gown, with a white mask dangling down the front of his chest. He was carrying a clipboard similar to the one the guard had.

He had a huge smile on his face as he extended his hand to Phillip, and then Maria. "Hi, you two! I hear you are going to be our next important scientists. Is that right?"

"We are definitely interested in science," Phillip said, taking in the sights before him, a little awed by what he was seeing.

"Very nice to meet you, Mr. Wright," Maria said. "Thanks for giving us some time."

"My pleasure. You are. . . .?"

"Oh," Maria said. "I'm Maria." She looked at Phillip. "And this is Phillip. We're on this project together."

"Well, welcome to my lab. Come on in." He ushered them back into the room from which he had just come. "You have questions, I am told."

"Yes, Mr. Wright. Just general stuff. Like something about your background and history, and how you got into this, and stuff like that."

They talked for quite awhile, and he told him about his schooling, and how he moved into his studies. After a while he said, "And I guess that brings us to where I am now." He moved over to a large table with pieces of what looked like rubber spread across some clear plastic sheets. Each sample had an identification number, and miscellaneous information printed on a piece of paper, such as the date of the experiment, and subsequent experiments.

He picked up one of the pieces. "This is the last piece of synthetic rubber I have been working with. I am trying to improve this and make it easy to produce. These are war times, and the government is trying all sorts of experiments to help the war effort." He picked up a large vial of liquid. "This is silicone oil, one of the main ingredients in making the synthetic rubber process. Something is missing from my formula to make this different. I just haven't found it yet."

Phillip pointed to several small vials of liquid. "What are those?"

"Just miscellaneous chemicals and acids I use for interactions. I haven't tried them all yet, but I will." He reached up for a small vial marked "Boric Acid" and examined it closely. "Hmmn," he murmured softly to himself. "This vial appears to have a crack or break in it, and . . . " At that moment, the vial came apart in his hand, and some of the liquid splashed into the vial of Silicone Oil. He quickly grabbed a rag and tried to mop up the mess, but as he did, he noticed that a chemical reaction was starting to happen inside the vial. He quickly put his arms out and gestured Phillip and Maria back. "Watch out, kids. I don't have any idea what is going to happen here. I don't want you to get hurt."

Phillip and Maria moved across the room and watched as the chemicals boiled, then subsided. Mr. Wright tentatively probed the mass of material that had formed in the bottom of the vial with a stainless steel spoon, then he put thick rubber gloves on. He reached in with great care and lifted the material out and set it on a large glass plate, where he began to mold the substance together. He was so intensely involved with the situation he seemed to have forgotten the presence of Maria and Phillip.

"What the - " he exclaimed. "Madison!" he called out to a man across the room. "Come here and look at this!" A dark-haired man with thick glasses walked quickly over and the two of them examined the material closely. "Madison, this stuff is amazing. It appears to look like rubber, but watch this!" He stretched the material and then let it go, and it snapped back to its original position. "Let's try this." He rolled a piece of the material into a ball and dropped it on the floor. To everyone's amazement, it bounced back up like a tennis ball. The two men were oblivious to anything or anyone else in their excitement.

"That's it," Maria said quietly to Phillip. "This is the moment that Silly Putty was discovered!"

Phillip nodded. "Yep. No doubt. Pretty cool!"

At that moment, Mr. Wright turned to the two of them. "Hey guys, I'm really sorry, but as you can see my hands are a bit full. You'll have to go now. Maybe we can meet again later sometime. Would that be O.K.?"

"No problem Mr. Wright. Thanks so much for talking to us. We'll let ourselves out." They both waved and then walked out the door into the corridor.

They talked excitedly as they moved toward the escalator.

"That was *so* cool!" Maria said.

Phillip's eyes were big. "Absolutely incredible. I can't believe we did this."

At the bottom they walked over to the desk and handed their Visitor tags to the guard.

Phillip was happy. "Thanks so much Sir. We really appreciate the visit."

"No problem, kids. I hope you get those A's. Come back and see us."

They left the building and walked around to the back of the parking lot.

"Well," Phillip said, smiling. "That was pretty much cool, but the trip itself was mind-blowing. Can you believe we traveled to the year 1943? We actually did it!"

They smiled at each other and walked over to the Discovery Machine and looked it over carefully. Maria reached out and touched as if seeing it for the first time. They smiled at each other in wonder, and climbed aboard. After buckling in, Phillip set the control time back for the present date in the future, and pushed the big button marked, "RETURN." The machine's gears whirred and trembled, and the craft vibrated softly as it began to fade from sight, moving slowly up and away from a parking lot in New Haven, Connecticut, in 1943.

As their craft slowly disappeared on its way home to the present, sometime in the future, Phillip and Maria smiled at each other. They were intuitively thinking and wondering where they might go on future travels, as they discovered why things are the way they are, and how they got that way, in a world full of incredible inventions and discoveries.

But as their vision blurred and the machine whirred around them, Phillip began thinking that it seemed so odd that this trip went off so easily. As if building a machine that would take them back in time was no big thing. Although this Silly Putty event was actually rather small as discoveries go, and the trip had happened so easily and quickly, the truth was that this small trip in time had actually been an astronomically huge achievement.

Phillip was still amazed that he had been able to put this together and had actually made it work. He secretly thought that a lot of what happened in his discovery came from sheer luck, and wondered if maybe many discoveries happened from luck, or things that happened spontaneously. This was in reality an event of incredible importance that reeked of ramifications for the future, and excitement and danger, not just for them, but maybe even for mankind itself. That was a scary thought, and Phillip felt humbled and suddenly very conscious of his age.

These thoughts weighed more heavily on his mind the more he thought about them. 'I'm almost fourteen,' Phillip thought. He thought about it some more. 'Actually, I'm *only* almost fourteen.' The more he thought about it, the more it seemed to startle him. The thought sent an old familiar shaft of fear down his spine, and he shivered slightly. He remembered when he had been much younger and would stand in his backyard at night staring up into the black starlit sky. He had been intensely frightened at the incredible immenseness and vastness of the sky above him, and felt overwhelmed with how insignificantly small he felt. It had scared him to think that his presence in this vastness could mean nothing. He remembered clearly wondering of what possible value his small pin speck of a life could have.

Everything about the Discovery Machine and these amazing trips to another time seemed to loom around his head like a dark cloud. He began to experience a nagging feeling of dread. And he knew that part of what he was feeling was that he had no idea where this seemingly innocent adventure would soon lead them.

If only he *could* have.

CHAPTER TWO: THE WHEEL

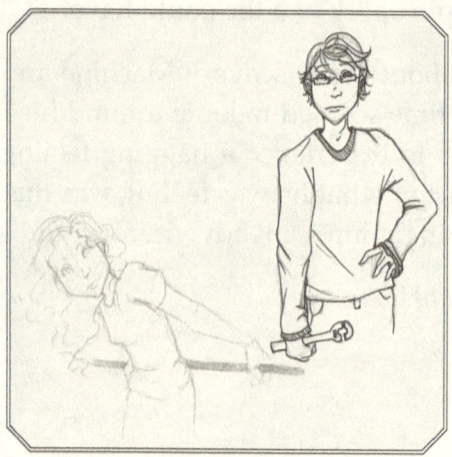

The exciting trip to the year 1943 that Phillip and Maria took had left them exhausted. When the machine returned them to Phillip's workroom, they realized that something in the process of traveling through time used an enormous amount of energy from their bodies. By the time they stepped down from the Discovery Machine and pulled the cover back over it, their legs and knees felt like butter. They walked wearily over to Phillip's couch, sat down, and instantly dropped off to sleep.

After about an hour's nap, they woke up hungry. Phillip said, "Let's go down to the kitchen and see what we can find in the refrigerator." They walked slowly downstairs and into the kitchen. Phillip opened the refrigerator and gazed inside. He closed the door again, and opened the cupboard.

"Dad's out of town for the weekend." He lifted a jar of peanut butter and a container of honey off the cupboard shelf, and put them on the counter. "Mom's showing houses and won't be back until late this afternoon. So I guess we're on our own." He pulled down a loaf of sourdough bread from the top of the refrigerator.

"Peanut butter and honey sandwiches O.K.?"

"Yup. I love them."

As Phillip started spreading the peanut butter onto the bread and pouring on the honey, Maria said, "I've been thinking. We've got to plan where we're going next, and I think that we just can't waste our time investigating modern day inventions like T.V. I mean, the invention of television was pretty amazing, but we need to make our searches more basic. More basic toward *original* thoughts."

He ripped off a paper towel from its roll, folded it over her sandwich, and handed it to her.

"I agree. You know, I was reading a story about Thomas Edison, the man who invented the light bulb - "

" - and a million other inventions too," Maria interrupted.

Phillip nodded and went on. "Apparently, Edison conducted over 1000 unsuccessful experiments in his efforts toward creating the light bulb. A news reporter once asked him if he considered the 1000 unsuccessful attempts to be failures. And do you know what Edison told him?"

Marie shook her head. "No. What?"

"He told him that the 1000 attempts were not failures, but that he had just found 1000 ways to *not* make a light bulb work."

Maria laughed. Phillip pulled a carton of milk out of the refrigerator and poured a bright red glass full for each for them. They sat down at the table and ate their sandwiches.

"I guess you might say that something you might try is only a failure until it works."

"So the moral might be to just keep on trying?"

"Yes. And believe in what you are doing so much that you have no doubts."

"Is that what we are doing?"

"I believe so."

They sat quietly, enjoying their sandwiches.

After a while, Maria got that fresh ready-for-anything look on her face that Phillip loved. "Well," she said turning back to the subject, "Any ideas?"

Her expression made him laugh. "Basic, huh?" He stared at the ceiling for a moment, as if trying to find some answer written up there in the rafters.

Then a smile came to his face slowly, like a bright candle being lit, and he said, "Well, you'll probably laugh, but how about the wheel?"

Maria's eyes brightened. "The wheel?"

"Yeah. I mean, we pretty much take the wheel for granted. It's on our cars, we use them to turn valves, and knobs, those circles are everywhere. But when the wheel was invented, it changed life for everyone from that point on. What do you think?"

"Mmmmmm," Maria said pensively. "That's good! Think about it. People were dragging things across the ground before the wheel. That's very cool, Phillip. Let's go see how it all happened."

"We've got a couple of hours before Mom gets back. You want to go now?"

But Maria was already skipping back upstairs toward the Discovery Machine, and pulling at the cover. They both pulled the cover off, and with a single agile spring she was up and into her co-pilot seat.

"C'mon, slow poke!"

Phillip laughed and jumped up onto the machine and into his chair. "Let's see. The wheel was invented sometime before recorded history. I'll have to set the controls on an approximate time-line search." He leaned forward, adjusted a dial, then typed onto the keyboard,

`Invention of the wheel.`

He turned to Maria. "Ready?"

"Yup. Let's do it!"

Phillip took a deep breath, brushed his hand over his glasses pushing them back on his face, paused with his hand held over the "TRAVEL" button, then pushed it.

The whirring of the gears started smoothly, and the machine started its familiar vibrations. They felt the machine starting to move, and the room began to go out of focus.

It seemed that they were in this state for a much longer time. The fleeting visions swirled around and across them sometimes gently, sometimes almost violently. Their craft shuddered and made new noises they had never heard before. Maria dug her right hand into the arm of her chair, and held on to Phillip's arm tightly, her lips pursed in a thin line across her mouth.

The surroundings came into focus and the machine rode in slowly to the ground. When it finally stopped vibrating, the time read-out on the screen monitor was strangely vague. It simply read,

`Pre-historic Man Era`

It didn't list a year or time, or for that manner, any other usable information.

The lack of help from the screen made Phillip grimace slightly. He pointed his finger at the screen and motioned for Maria to look.

"Very interesting," she said, twisting her mouth in the manner she always did when she was speculating about anything.

They quickly jumped down and walked over to the edge of the ridge where the machine had landed. Still apprehensive from the incredible experience of arriving on the Discovery Machine, they dropped to their knees and peered slowly over the edge.

Below them, a broad valley below stretched between two low ranges of hills. Not over 75 or 80 yards away, they saw what appeared to be a small community of people. The scene had the appearance of being agricultural, because in the distance they could see what appeared to be small patches of soil that had obviously been hand-worked and planted with some type of vegetation. Scattered logs and small trees were lying about on the ground. On the back of the clearing, leaning up against the ridge wall, were what looked like crude spears and other handmade weapons.

"Well," Phillip whispered, "from what I've read, this community seems to be a little more advanced than the era of the 'Hunter-Gatherer', where the men hunted live game, and women would gather wild vegetation from what grew in the area. This group has apparently learned about planting and growing seeds. A big step."

Maria was intently studying the scene below. She whispered softly to Phillip. "It looks like they have also learned more about weapons." She was staring. "Well, all I can say is that the expression, 'stepping back in time' has a whole new meaning to me all of a sudden." She caught her breath and pointed. "Look!"

Phillip followed her pointed finger.

On the edge of the clearing below, a long-haired bearded man, roughly clad in what appeared to be animal skins, was dragging a wrapped object of some type with great effort across the ground. The object was tied to the center of two long poles, and the man held one end of both of the poles in his hands, and dragging the other behind him, which left a trail of deep grooves behind on the ground.

"That is a travois. Even our Native Americans used it to carry things. Well, it's obvious *that* guy doesn't know about the wheel yet," Phillip observed wryly.

"Phillip, look over there at that fire pit. It's just like I read about in the encyclopedia. See those long tree sections in the fire? Before man really learned to make fire, he would just keep a master fire burning. See how those trees are lying over the edge of the fire? As the end of each log burns, they just push the log further into the fire, moving it a bit at a time until the entire log has been burned."

"Hmmmm," Phillip murmured. "That's actually pretty efficient, except I guess someone has to tend the fire all the time."

Just then a man walked up to the fire pit and stood looking down at the logs. He appeared to be studying a section of tree that had one end broken off cleanly. The other end had been slowly burning off. What was left was a section of log about two feet in diameter, and about three feet long.

The man placed his foot on the log and began rocking it back and forth, until he lost control of it, and it suddenly rolled out of the pit and began slowly rolling down the slight slope. The man followed; seemingly fascinated by the way it was moving. Every time the log would stop, he would push it slightly until it started rolling again.

Maria smiled at Phillip.

"I think he's got the idea," Phillip said. "Let's see what he does with it."

They watched the man as he played with and studied the log. With what looked like a sharp-edged rock of some type, he whacked at the burned area on that end of the log until it was fairly flat like the other end of the log, which had broken off cleanly. After a while he left and returned with two thick round pieces of branches, which he sharpened with some type of a cutting tool, and then pounded into the opposite ends of the log.

"My gosh, Phillip," Maria whispered, taking in the excitement of the moment, "that's an axle! This guy has just created the first axle!"

The man then brought two long poles over, notched their ends slightly behind the ends, and lashed these poles at the notched points onto the two sticks he had pounded into the log.

He then lashed two more short pieces of stick across the long poles in the approximate center of their length, and covered the area between these sticks with a piece of hide. He picked up the poles and tentatively pulled the contraption toward him. It rolled easily, and you could see the delight in his eyes even from the distance where Phillip and Maria were watching above. They were sharing the excitement.

"Wow!" Maria said. "That guy is *smart!*"

"Yeah," Phillip replied. "I wonder if he has any idea of what he has just done."

The man was pulling his rolling machine behind him with the poles, and a crowd was beginning to gather, pointing and talking loudly about the new machine. Someone placed a small child on the hide and you could hear the child's delighted squeals as the man pulled on the poles.

Maria was pondering what she was seeing.

"You know, Phillip, this kind of eliminates the idea that people of earlier times couldn't think at the level we do, doesn't it? I mean, we just assume that because we are supposed to be the most advanced culture yet, that we are also the most intelligent. Do you think that maybe intelligence is more basic than just being part of a modern culture?

"Yep. That makes sense to me, too."

Then Phillip was caught up in the dramatics of the moment. "And there you have it, Madame," he gestured with a flair and a melodramatic bow. "The invention of the wheel! And we saw it happen!"

Maria smiled at Phillip's corny comments and gestures, but she was still studying the scene below.

"I suppose we had better get back now Phillip, but there is another thing we have seen here that we should probably look into for the next time.

Phillip was immediately interested. "What have we seen here besides the discovery of the wheel?"

Maria said quietly, "*Fire*, Phillip. Pretty basic. How *did* men first discover fire, and how did they handle it?"

As they reluctantly left the amazing scene behind, and walked back toward the Discovery Machine, they were both already thinking about how their next adventure of finding out about *fire* would come about.

Back aboard the machine and seated comfortably in their red velvet easy chairs, Phillip pushed the "RETURN" button. They waited for their vibrating travel machine to take them home, back to a time where no one thought about *how* wheels came about. A time where people were into *using* inventions, and not *creating* them. And great inventions that people take for granted, not aware how others had worked and studied so diligently for them to even exist.

'What a shame,' Phillip thought to himself as the machine began to fade back into the future. 'There is so much excitement in discovery. Everything we do and everything we have is a result of some person thinking through a new thought, a new thought that would make life easier for those who follow. We seldom even take the time to think how these discoveries came about. How *can* we ignore this?'

He leaned his head back against the chair and closed his eyes. The two young explorers slowly faded into another time.

Chapter Three: Fire

It had been a week since they had seen the wheel being dis-covered. It was early the next Saturday morning, and Phillip was waiting for Maria to arrive. He was working on the dial set-tings on the Discovery Machine for the upcoming trip to see how fire was discovered. Phillip's dad was in the garage working in his woodshop, and his mother was already in the field showing homes in her job as a realtor.

Maria had called Phillip late at night in the middle of the week, and they had talked for more than two hours about what they had been through.

"Phillip," she had said, "how are *you* handling all this? I mean, this is really very hard for me to believe, even though I know we have done it. We are not talking about some world famous Einstein doing this. *You and I,* two *ninth-graders* for Pete's sake, have actually taken *two* trips to *some other time* on this planet! We have seen things happen, historical things, that *absolutely no one alive today could even imagine.* I come at home at night, sit down at my desk to do homework and pinch myself to keep from shouting about it through the windows. And I'll tell you, it is really hard to keep interested in math problems after you've seen someone invent the wheel." She laughed.

"Phillip, this is all making me a little nuts, and it still scares the heck out of me, but I can hardly wait to do it again and take another trip on that machine."

"Yeah, Maria," he had replied, "Me too. I can hardly wait. I also can hardly think about anything else. My folks have noticed my weirdness and think I am totally freaked out. My mom actually called Mrs. Pearson, *our* teacher, to see if something at school is bothering me. Mom hasn't asked about anything yet, but I do see her giving me some strange glances."

There had been a long moment of silence. "Maria," he said softly, you have to promise me that if this gets too intense for you to handle, you'll let me know, and I'll back off a bit." He grimaced, and hesitantly added, ". . . or even stop."

"No way! Phillip, you'll *never* hear me asking you to let up. This is absolutely the most exciting thing that has ever happened to me, *and* to you. We *have* to see it through. This may not be just about some incredible adventure for two ninth graders. Don't you believe that? You *have* to believe that!"

Maria's words had burned a hole in his brain. The night was restless, and he felt his focus intensify. He was up early.

Phillip heard a knock at the front door, so he went to the window and leaned out. Maria was standing on the porch looking up toward his window with an expectant look on her face.

"Come on up," Phillip called.

Maria entered the room carrying a small thermos and a brown bag. "Sandwiches and cocoa," she said in answer to the unspoken question in Phillip's eyes. "I thought we might need them this time."

"Good thinking. Makes me hungry already." He reached out for the bag and started to stick his hand inside to explore.

She slapped his hand. "Not until later, silly."

They climbed up on the Discovery Machine and Maria peeked over his shoulder at what he was doing with the dials.

"What do you think?"

"I think we'll have to go back a lot further this time. I'll have to set it for another ATL search."

"ATL?"

"Approximate Time Line. This will probably take us back to very early man, maybe even before Cro-Magnon man. And considering the fact that man did not communicate very well, or at all, with any other people outside his own tribe in those days, the Discovery Machine may be sending us to different places for different experiences. We just don't know who or even when someone actually took credit for discovering a method for starting a fire."

"Well," Maria said with the quirky little twist of her mouth, "when you think about it, there are really many ways to start a fire that *we* know about, not even considering that of using matches."

"Exactly."

"And they probably didn't all get discovered at the same time, or at the same place, or by the same people."

"That's right."

"So, I wonder how the Discovery Machine will handle this."

"I guess there is only one way to find out. It's 9:30 a.m. We've got the whole day to explore."

Phillip glanced over all the dials and gears again. He looked at Maria, who was sitting with her hands locked together and a huge smile on her face hovered over by very wide open eyes, flashing with excitement. He laughed. "You set?"

"Yup. All set. Contact. Clear. Prop on. Vamanos. 10-4. Let's do it!"

Phillip laughed, and pushed the "TRAVEL" with a dramatic flair like that of a concert pianist.

The vibration of the machine seemed to last even longer this time, and the speed of the gears changed, speeding up, then slowing down again. Finally, all of the mechanisms slowed down as the surroundings came into focus, and finally stopped after they glided softly to the ground.

"Look on the screen, Maria," Phillip said.

Maria leaned unbuckled her belt and leaned over his shoulder. The screen read,

```
Alternative solutions. Return to DM
    immediately after this event.
```

They looked at each other for a moment taking that in.

It was very cold. Phillip reached in a compartment and pulled out two jackets and caps and handed a set to Maria.

"I figured we would be needing these today."

"Thanks," Maria said as she put her jacket on and fitted her cap to her head. She picked up the sandwich bag and tucked the thermos under her arm, and they jumped down to the ground.

Vivid orange and red streaks of early morning sun cut across the sky through a light haze of wispy clouds. The machine had landed behind a small grassy knoll. They walked down a long slope and saw that beneath the knoll was a large clearing about 100 yards in width. The clearing backed up against a dark cliff, which ran about a half mile in length. At various spots in the bottom of this cliff were several natural caves. In front of each cave was a large cleared area where a large fire pit was being tended by at least one person from each of these caves.

Phillip and Maria crouched down to keep out of sight. There was other activity going on, with people clad in fur walking in and out of the caves, carrying things, and several groups of people seated or standing talking with each other.

"We're going to have to get closer," Phillip whispered. "I can't make out anything that's happening."

"Be careful," Maria whispered back, as they began to edge across the ground toward the edge of the cliffs.

They worked their way carefully down the hill and over to where there was a small opening in the cliff that would allow them clearer vision to the scene below without too much danger of being discovered.

"Look, Phillip. Those fire pits are not using trees and branches like the one we saw on our last trip."

"Yeah. So I guess we can assume this *is* an earlier approach to the use of fire."

It was getting colder, and they huddled closer to stay warm. Maria remembered the thermos.

"How about some hot chocolate?"

"You bet!"

She unscrewed the top and poured the lid full of chocolate. She took a short sip and handed the cup to Phillip.

"Hmmmm, good," he said.

They sat quietly, passing the cup of chocolate back and forth, watching the scene below them.

"Phillip, what's that guy doing?"

"What guy?"

"There." She pointed to a man sitting on the edge of the nearest fire pit. In his lap was a flat piece of wood. He had a round limb branch about a foot long in his hand, and he was rubbing one end of this stick across the face of the flat piece of wood, apparently trying to smooth it and shape the end of the stick and make it round. He was bearing down pretty hard on the wood, and rubbing it harder and faster.

Suddenly he stopped and leaned down closely to look at the wood. He reached out with his finger and carefully touched the area where he was rubbing. The instant his finger came in contact with the wood he jerked it back in surprise, then jumped up blowing on his finger to cool it off.

He called out and another man ran out of the cave and rushed over to him. The man in the fire pit motioned for the other man to sit. Once again he started rubbing the two pieces of wood in the same manner. After a few minutes, he grabbed the other man's finger and pressed it on the surface of the wood. The man shouted loudly and jerked his hand back, and he also began blowing on his finger to cool it off.

Maria looked over at Phillip, her eyes wide with pleasure.

The two men talked and gestured back and forth excitedly, both tentatively reaching out and touching the wood, then examining their fingers. The fire pit man seemed very intrigued and began rubbing the stick across the wood again in an almost feverish pitch. After a few moments, a slender column of smoke began to come up from the wood. The man jumped up and held the wood outstretched in his hands, watching it until it stopped smoking. He stood up and walked around the fire circle, glancing at the two pieces of wood frequently. He sat down next to the pieces and studied them for a very long time. The other man finally walked back into the cave.

After a long time studying the wood pieces and looking at them very carefully, the man picked up the stick, re-set the larger piece of wood on his lap, and after taking a very visible deep breath, began to rub the stick against the wood with a great ferociousness. In a few minutes the wood starting smoking again, but this time the man kept on rubbing. He leaned over and began to blow on the wood. He seemed possessed.

Suddenly, to his obvious surprise, a tiny flame spurted out weakly. He quickly reached down and picked up some very small pieces of wood splinters and tiny twigs, and dropped them on the small fire. To his visible delight, the small flame caught up with the twigs and surged to life. He quickly placed the flat piece of wood on the ground in the fire pit, and started adding more and more pieces of wood to it, until soon he had a raging fire.

He called out again, this time more urgently, and the other man came running out of the cave and over to the pit, where they both started pointing excitedly at the fire. Other people started spilling out of the cave, and soon others from the other caves were there surrounding the raging fire in the fire pit.

Maria and Phillip were bouncing up and down in excitement over what they had just seen. But at that very moment, one of the men coming out of the cave happened to glance up and catch their movements, and stopped in his tracks to stare at them.

They froze.

The man grabbed the arm of another man, spun him around, and pointed toward Phillip and Maria.

Now hunched over, Phillip whispered,

"Let's get out of here, now!"

They eased back away from the opening, and scrambled frantically back up toward the knoll where the Discovery Machine was resting. They heard an increasing commotion of voices behind them. Phillip grabbed Maria's hand and they scrambled frantically, slipping and stumbling up the steep slope, dislodging stones which cascaded down the slope behind them. Phillip tripped over a rock and hit the ground hard with his face, drawing blood instantly. Maria grabbed him by the arm and pulled him to his feet.

The voices behind them became even louder, and as they glanced back over their shoulders, in their horror they saw that a group of men had reached the edge of the clearing, and upon spotting them, lunged violently toward them with spears and clubs flailing, emitting horrible shouting noises. Phillip and Maria couldn't move their feet. They watched in growing fear as the men charged up the hill toward them.

"Come on!" Phillip screamed and grabbed at Maria's arm, but in doing so, he lost his footing again and they both fell to the ground. Maria cried out. They struggled trying to regain their footing, not noticing that two of the men had gone around them and over the top of the hill above them. A spear pierced the ground next to Maria's head, and then another bounced off a rock to one side of Phillip. With a strength that came from a need for survival somewhere deep within them, the two children pulled themselves up together, and scrambled in the loose gravel for the top of the hill. They reached the top, rounded the knoll and stopped in cold paralyzed terror. Standing between them and the Discovery Machine were the two men, frozen in place in front of the machine, staring at it, holding large brutal looking clubs in their hands. The other men caught up with them, and as they reached the top and saw the machine, they appeared stunned by the strange apparition in front of them, and several of them rocked back on their heels in shock. Phillip and Maria took in the horrifying spectacle of the circle of armed primitive men around them. Their hearts beat wildly and their eyes met in terror as they realized the reality of the situation.

They were surrounded.

CHAPTER FOUR: MORE FIRE

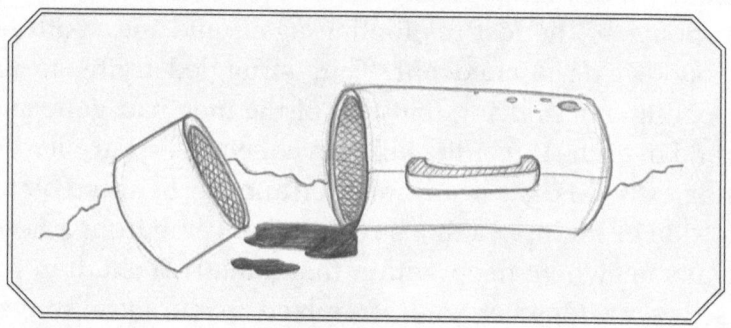

It was somewhere in prehistoric time, and time suddenly meant nothing. But at that moment, there were two levels of shock for everyone there as they all stood at the top of the hill. The children were terrified at being surrounded and being threatened with death, and the men were completely frightened and dumfounded at the apparition of a strange structure before them. Two of the men now lay face down with their arms out in front of them in a totally submissive posture toward the Discovery Machine, and others of the men held their hands in front of them, obviously afraid to look at the machine. The men all began to drop slowly to their knees in front of the machine.

"Phillip," Maria whispered. "Look!" They glanced around at the men all now prone on the ground facing the machine. Her voice crackled with hoarseness from fear. "They're not even looking at us!"

Phillip took Maria's hand and whispered back, "Move slowly with me. Let's try and make it to the DM."

Step by step they moved past the men toward the machine. They heard a low growling murmur from one of the men and froze.

"Don't move!" Phillip whispered. "Maria," he said as quietly as he could manage, "Turn your head slowly and see what's happening behind us."

Maria slowly turned her head and stood like a rock. She turned back equally as slowly. "Two of them are looking at us, but they seem really scared. Let's keep going."

They eased past the two remaining men to the edge of the DM, and grabbed onto the grips on the side.

Phillip whispered, "It's now or never. Are you ready?" Maria squeezed his hand, and whispered back, "yes."

Phillip said, "on three." He counted, "one", "two", "THREE!" They jumped on the machine. Without sitting down, Phillip punched the button below the screen, which was now calmly reading,

```
Proceed Next.
```

They dived into the chairs, hands gripping the arms as the gears engaged and the machine began to vibrate. As they began to lift off, Phillip glanced over at Maria to see her scrunched up in her chair, eyes crunched together, her fingers digging into the fabric of the chair. Then he stole a look at the men, who were now on their feet. But as the sound of the whirring of the machine increased, the men again backed away, frightened at the foreign sound and the incredible vision before them. Maria was pleading softly aloud, trying to make the machine go faster. "C'mon, C'mon, C'mon, COME ON!"

And then they were gone.

It seemed that time stopped, but after what seemed like only a few moments later, after ominous sounds from the machine, it once again came to a gliding stop.

They were still trying to gather their breath from the terror of their narrow escape, and they glanced around apprehensively. Phillip leaned over and checked the screen.

"No other message here, Maria. Maybe this will be the last stop on this trip."

"Phillip," Maria was still breathing hard. She looked at his face and said with a shaky voice, "You're bleeding pretty badly from that cut. Hold still and I'll clean it." She reached in the locker, brought out a small plastic bottle of water, and swabbed the cut with a piece of paper towel.

Maria's hands shook badly as she cleaned his wound, and when finally satisfied the bleeding had stopped, she gathered up the paper towel and threw it in the bin below the locker. A tear began to cut a line down her face, and she sat looking at Phillip. He put his arms around her and she lay her head on his shoulder, and began to cry softly.

"Oh, Phillip, I was so scared." They sat closely for a long time, quietly, not saying a word. Phillip held her tightly.

Still a little wide-eyed and apprehensive, they began looking around to see where they were. This time, the Discovery Machine had landed on a small grassy clearing. About 100 yards away was the edge of a very large body of water. Large waves were breaking on the shore. They jumped down and walked over to the edge of the clearing and looked at the water.

"Looks like an ocean," Maria stated, matter-of-factly, somewhat calmer now.

"Looks like it to me too. But which one, and where is it, and *when?*"

"Was there anything at all on the screen?"

Phillip shook his head. "No instructions, no warnings, *or* dates and times."

As they began to look more closely around the area, they began to hear what sounded like voices coming from a group of trees just off the beach. They looked at each other.

"Do you hear that?" Maria asked.

Phillip nodded. "It seems to be coming from behind that grove of trees over there."

He put his hand on her shoulder and looked into her eyes. "Are you o.k.? Should we go home?"

She touched his hand and returned a brave smile. "No, I'm all right. Now." She took a deep breath and looked around. "We're here now. Let's see what this is all about."

"O.k. But you'll let me know if you feel we need to go, right?"

She nodded.

They crept very slowly and cautiously toward the sounds and into a small stand of trees and heavy brush, ready to stop and run at any moment. The sounds were getting stronger as they made their way through the trees and brushes and approached what appeared to be a small clearing in the woods. Crouching down, they crept up to the edge of the clearing. Slowly parting the leaves of a small fan palm, they could see several women seated in a circle on the ground around a larger and older woman who seemed to be the leader of the group.

As Phillip and Maria watched, the woman would one by one hold up to the light small chunks of what appeared to be clear and colored glass from a collection resting on her lap on a piece of animal fur of some type. Every time she held up a different piece of glass toward the sun, the other women in the group would murmur with appreciation.

The woman then picked up an especially beautiful clear stone and held it up, examining it with great care. After looking at it closely, she set it down on a small stand of lashed of fabric and twigs next to her on the ground, about a foot tall, obviously tied to hold the stones for display.

As she and the other women talked and gestured, the sun appeared brightly from behind a cloud, and a strong ray of direct sunlight beamed down directly into the clearing and onto the piece of glass. Unnoticed by any of the group, a small wisp of smoke began to appear in the leaves below the stone, where a single ray of intense light was focused.

One of the women suddenly noticed the smoke and stood up abruptly. She pointed to the smoke and began shouting. All the women jumped up and ran over to the smoking leaves and began jumping up and down, pointing and shouting all at the same time.

In an instant, a small puff of flame ignited in the leaves. This terrified the women and they immediately ran away screaming. Except for the leader. She remained, somewhat taken aback, but nonetheless intensely fascinated by the small fire. She bent down and cleared some area around the small fire to keep it from spreading, and then crouched down to study what was happening closely.

She picked up the piece of glass and again held it toward the sun, studying it. Then she held it above her hand and moved it up and down focusing the bright spot that appeared on her palm. As she felt heat on her flesh, she moved it away quickly. She did this again and again. She squinted her eyes, and an odd smile of satisfaction spread across her face.

Phillip touched Maria on her shoulder and motioned for her to follow him away from the clearing. They quietly left the area and finally walked out of the small stand of trees back to the beach and the Discovery Machine.

On the way they talked. "That was pretty cool", Maria said. "The way that woman's eyes lit up when she figured out why the leaves caught fire."

"Yeah, it *was* cool. Also, it made me think. It's obvious that in some discoveries, there may be more than one idea involved, and more than one way to make the discovery work. I mean, we saw two completely different methods found for starting a fire. There may actually have been many more."

"Yup," Maria said. "You know, we haven't talked about it at all, but don't you think that until times like in these discoveries, mostly men just brought pieces of wood to their caves and campsites that were already burning, like from lightning strikes?"

"Un huh," Phillip reflected. "Can you imagine how important it must have been to tend a fire and make it keep burning all the time, through all weather conditions? Someone had to be responsible all hours of the day and night to keep the fire going. And when it *did* go out for some reason, they had to either go to a fire somewhere else and bring back a piece of burning wood, or wait until some storm caused another lightning strike, so they could find yet another piece of burning wood. Fire must have been really important to the survival of these early people." He thought about it briefly. "And letting a fire go out would probably be a serious event, even a *crime*."

They had reached the Discovery Machine and were leaning back against it, looking at the ocean. Maria was being very quiet.

"O.K.," Phillip said. "I can tell you're perplexed about something. What is it?"

"The thermos," she said. "When we had to run from the first observation spot I didn't have time to grab it, and left it there. I just wonder what those people will make of it."

"Good thought." Phillip pondered that for a moment. "Me too." They looked at each other briefly.

They climbed up onto the machine and sat back in their seats. Phillip checked the screen and it now read,

```
More solutions possible.
Event complete for this date.
```

He reached over and wearily punched the "RETURN" button, and then they settled back into the comfort of their chairs, closing their eyes as the familiar vibrations increased.

'Two events were a lot for one day,' Maria thought. 'Especially one of them.' She shuddered slightly remembering their fear and the chase, and felt herself slipping away.

"I wonder where we'll go next.'

The thought had scarcely left her mind, and she was asleep.

CHAPTER FIVE: RE-CALCULATING

They arrived back a Phillip's workroom just in time to hear his dad calling from downstairs. Maria stirred to life. They jumped down from the machine, which was still whining softly, winding down from the trip, and quickly covered it with the blanket. Phillip ran over to the door.

"Dad!" he called down. "Did you want me?"

"Is Maria up there with you? What are you guys doing?"

"Yes. She's up here. Uhh, we're doing homework. Did you need me for anything?"

"No, I just wanted to know if you were up there. I'm going downtown to the hardware store for a few things. You two behave yourselves while I'm gone. Mom will be home later."

"O.K." Phillip called out. The front door closed shut. Phillip looked at Maria sheepishly.

"Well, if that wasn't lying, it was pretty close to it. Makes me feel a little guilty. But I guess we could say that we really are study-ing geography and history, and even physics."

"And maybe a little social sciences thrown in," Maria said.

They walked downstairs and into the kitchen. Phillip filled his mother's brass teapot with water and put it on the burner.

"How about some hot chocolate?"

"Sure", Maria said pensively. "You know, Phillip, didn't you think it kind of strange that the machine didn't take us to a place where people were using flint stones to start fires? I mean, *that* is the most obvious method that historians talk about. And I have read about that being the method that finally brought about the manufacture of matches, which uses the same principle of abra-sion and friction to create sparks or fire."

"Yeah, that is a little strange. But maybe that's not the way the machine calculates and reasons. Maybe it doesn't seek out the obvious solutions all the time. Remember the wheel example that we saw? There are sure to be other possibilities, including one I read about in a science magazine using board slats bound together and then cut in a circle. Even though I put this machine together, I still haven't worked out all the details of how it actu-ally calculates a destination." He pulled out two cups and loaded them with powdered chocolate.

"And I've got another thought for *you*. Did you ever notice in all those sci-fi movies about time machines how when the machine went on a trip and arrived on a scene, it just seemed to magically land in an open area? Doesn't that stretch your imagination a bit? Doesn't it seem just a bit too convenient? Well, I think the authors of those stories took the easy route in creating their plots. I mean, why wouldn't the time machine in those movies ever land imbed-ded in the middle of a building, or a lake, or any number of pos-sible dangerous places?"

Maria looked at him quizzically. She thoughtfully reached in the refrigerator and pulled out a container of half and half and held it in front of him for approval.

"You mind? It tastes richer this way."

"No. That sounds good. Go for it. Me too. "Thanks. I mean, I think we've been lucky ourselves with our trips to the discoveries so far. A couple of them were in prehistoric times, and the odds of materializing near a man-made structure were pretty slim. Even the 1943 trip was in a fairly rural area. And the machine knows how to come home safely to my workroom. But I've been thinking that the more we take trips toward modern times, the more chances we might have of having the Discovery Machine materializing in a location already occupied by some structure or building. That could be dangerous and even disastrous. How can we possibly know what may or may not be built where we are trying to materialize? What if we were to materialize inside a building, or even in the walls themselves? We could be killed. I've got to think about this seriously before we take another trip."

He turned off the burner and poured hot water into the cups. Maria poured in the cream and stirred the chocolate. She handed Phillip one of the cups, and they walked out to the front porch and sat on the swing together, watching the street. There was a nice breeze blowing through the trees, and there was a pair of sparrows busily building a nest in the edge of the roof at the end of the porch.

They sat there for quite a while without talking, thinking, and watching the nesting birds. They savored the sweet pungent chocolate. It was very calming. Then Maria turned and said,

"Phillip, we're talking about *density* here."

"Density?"

"Yup. Isn't any structure, or any object, or even a person for that matter, just a huge collection of atoms bound together in one place? The tighter they are, the more dense they are. There is even density in air, although we can breathe it and move around in it easily without problems. Water is another form of density. We can move around in it also, although not as easily as air, and we sure can't breath in it. Something like wood, or steel, or even dirt, is much more dense, and would be impossible for us to move *or* breathe in."

"I think I know where you're going with this. If I were able to build into the machine a sensing ability to detect *levels* of density, and implement a system that would enable the Discovery Machine to avoid areas of density other than air, then we could *avoid* the materialization dangers."

"Exactly!" Maria smiled.

"Maria, you are *very* clever. Especially for a *girl*." She poked him in the ribs. He thought quietly for a few minutes. Then his eyes lit up. "How about if we go a step further?"

"Further?"

"What if I also built in a delay for the final materialization moment? If I can delay the final moment of materialization, we would still be out of focus to anyone that might be in the area. We could see them but they couldn't see us. We would be invisible!"

"Wow! I like that!" Maria was excited. "That would also allow us to position ourselves wherever we wanted *before* we became visible. We could even appear *inside* a group of people without them sensing our presence, and we could certainly find hiding places if we needed to." She looked at Phillip incredulously. "You can do that?"

Phillip scratched his head in thought. "I think I know how to make the adjustments to the DM, but it's going to take me the rest of the week to scrounge up some components. Can you make it over here next Saturday?"

Maria nodded. "Yup. That's a definite affirmative. How about around 9:30, and I'll bring lunch and hot chocolate again. In the meantime, we can talk at school. That O.K.?"

"I'll be ready."

"Maria handed him her empty cup and stepped off the porch. She smiled back over her shoulder and blew Phillip a kiss, and then stopped and turned around and faced him.

"You know, Phillip, I love being with you and doing this. It's really cool."

Phillip smiled back. Then he waved, opened the door, and went in.

CHAPTER SIX: THE SHADOW

Maria was sitting on a bench in the outside school patio, waiting to share lunch with Phillip. As usual, she was reading a book. As she turned the pages, she felt she was being watched. She glanced up and to her right to find herself in the fixed stare of a very husky ninth grade girl she had seen around the campus. Her name was Moana. Maria had noticed her many times around the school. She always seemed to be nearby.

Moana was a tall and husky brunette with straight black hair that came down past her shoulders. She was as a tall as most tenth and eleventh graders, and large-boned and athletic. Her clothes were always clean, but she wore only plain jeans and pullovers. Moana seldom smiled, and seemed to be threatening in her mannerisms. She kept mostly to herself, and didn't appear to have other friends. Maria didn't just didn't know how to take her. Maria smiled tentatively at Moana, but her expression didn't change, and Moana directed her gaze elsewhere with an air of feigned indifference.

At that moment, Phillip walked up and sat down beside Maria on the bench.

"Hey, you," he said affectionately. "What's happening?"

Maria focused on Phillip with a sense of comfortable relief. "Hi back," she said, and reached over and touched him on his sleeve. "Not much. Just reading."

Phillip craned his neck around to see the title of the book Maria was reading. "Hmmmm," he said pensively. "'*The Territorial Imperative*.' What's that all about?"

"It's a book I dug out of my mother's library that she read when she was in college. It's pretty interesting. It's about *wolves*, actually."

"Wolves?"

"Yes. And how they act as a family unit." She turned slightly and faced Phillip. "Did you know wolves have a very defined internal pecking order of authority? They are extremely intelligent. They have a main dominant leader, and then essentially a hierarchy of the most powerful to the weakest. They even have a social structure with well-defined rules, and assigned punishments for any family member who breaks any of the rules, ranging from physical abuse to banishment from the family. One of the main focuses of the book appears to be the similarities to humans."

"No way."

"Yes, way," Maria smiled. "But what I thought was the most interesting so far about the book was the way the author did the studies and research."

"What did he do?"

"The author's name was Richard Aubrey. What Aubrey did was to move into the territory of an existing family of wolves and actually *live with them*. I guess it took a long time to gain their acceptance. He moved around mostly on all fours. It was amazing to me that they did in fact eventually allow him to be a member of their family. He hunted with them, he ate with them, he did everything with them."

"Wow." Phillip said. "That *is* amazing." He thought about it briefly. "I bet he came back to human society a little wild."

"Yeah," Maria said, laughing lightly. "Can you *imagine* coming back to our human civilization after total exposure to the wild for all that time?" She pursed her lips, thinking. "I bet taking a shower was a real experience after icy cold mountain streams." She put a marker in her book and closed it.

"Maria," Phillip said, with a change in tone, "When I came up to the bench, you had an expression on your face that was a little strange. What were you thinking about?"

"Oh," Maria replied, a little subdued. "Do you know that Samoan girl, Moana?" She motioned with her head toward where Moana was sitting. "Take a good look. She's big, and looks a little unfriendly. You might have noticed her. Have you seen her around before this?"

Phillip looked, and then tapped his finger on the bench. "Yep. I have. I've seen her a lot. It's strange you should mention this. I've had the feeling that she is shadowing us."

"Shadowing us?"

"Yes. She never seems to get very close, but I always see her around us here at school. Do you think she's up to something?"

"I don't know. I've tried to be friendly, but she just doesn't respond. I wonder what her story is."

"You know," Phillip said, "The Samoan culture is very much about being a warrior, and ferociousness, and all that. From what I've read, they are an extremely proud people, and not people to be pushed around. Maybe we'll find out someday."

He smiled and pulled his lunch sack out of his backpack. "Mom is a nut for Lingonberry Jam."

Maria's eyes sparkled with amusement. "And. . . .?"

"*And*, she made us some great Lingonberry Jam and Peanut Butter sandwiches on fresh homemade nut bread. You want to share?"

"Sounds scrumptious. And *I* made some sandwiches out of my mom's Italian meatloaf. I *know* they're good. How about half and half?"

They ate quietly together, chatting about their projects with the Discovery Machine, and family, and school, until the warning bell sounded. When they stood up to walk to their next class, they looked over to where Moana had been sitting. She was nowhere to be seen.

CHAPTER SEVEN: SAN FRANCISCO

It was a little after 9:00 a.m. the next Saturday morning. Phillip's parents were both gone again, and he was eager to get started on their next trip together. Phillip was feeling more confident since he made the adjustments to the DM, and he hummed quietly to himself as he made final trip adjustments to the gauges and valves, and prepared to type in the travel directions.

As he finished the entry, he heard Maria at the door. He shouted out the window, "Come on up!"

Maria bounced up the stairs and into Phillip's room, and set a bag of sandwiches and a new thermos on the table.

"Boy, am I ready for this one!" She was exuberant and glowing with excitement. She came nearer and looked closely at Phillip's head. "Phillip, that cut is better, but it's still red and angry. Are you taking care of it?"

"It's O.K.," Phillip said, nonchalantly. I put some stuff on it." He motioned toward the DM. "Now I think we can pursue discoveries made in later time periods, and in more populated area without worrying about internal collisions. So, where would you like to go first?"

Maria could hardly contain herself. "Well, you'll probably laugh, but I've always been fascinated over how jeans and Levis came about, especially since that's about all I ever wear. So, I've done a little Research," she smiled coquettishly, "And found out that a 20-year-old east coast merchant by the name of Levi Strauss developed the first Levis pants during the Gold Rush in northern California in 1850. He shipped large containers of dry goods all the way from New York to set up a new business, and shipped more later. He was catering to the needs of the California gold miners, who apparently were a pretty desperate group of men, existing in a really unpleasant environment with few creature comforts, or even bare working essentials." Maria could hardly contain herself. "*And*, since we know the exact time and location of Levi Strauss' arrival to northern California, I think it would be fun to watch him arriving, and see how he actually came up with the concept of making these pants." She looked at Phillip excitedly. "What do you think?"

"I like it." Phillip smiled at her excitement and pushed his glasses back up on his nose, from where they always seemed to be slipping.

"Also", Maria added slyly, "since we now have a way to arrive on a scene without being detected, I suggest we dress up as much as we can with clothes of that time period so we can walk about freely without arousing suspicion."

"That'll work. But I guess we can't wear jeans, huh?'

"Obviously not a good choice for pants."

"Maybe just some dark cotton pants for me like the ones you're wearing. I have a pair in the closet. We can take sweaters to go over our shirts."

They opened the closet and Phillip pulled out a dark pair of trousers, went into the bathroom, and put them on. Maria was already on the DM when he came out.

She smiled down at him. "I also brought this small backpack, which I think will fit in as far as looks go." She looked at him and smiled. "They had backpacks in those days. I already put the food and hot chocolate in it. And if the visit time element is anything like our last trips, I don't think we'll be there long enough to worry about coming up with currency of the time period to make food or other purchases." She tapped her finger on the desk dramatically. "Well, *I'm* ready to go. How about *you*?"

Phillip hopped up on the DM and went over to the keyboard. "You know, Maria, sometimes you amaze me."

Maria smiled and handed him a piece of paper. "You're just saying that because it's true."

Phillip laughed. "Yup, that must be it."

"These are the time and location details for your entry."

"Thanks, clever girl."

Phillip read the notes on the paper carefully, then, leaning forward, he typed in the words, on the keyboard,

```
San Francisco, northern California,

   March, 1853, Enter Levi Strauss.
```

He settled back in his chair, and motioned to Maria to buckle in as he did the same. "Maria, these trips will be a little different from now on. Our arrivals at different scenes will be completely different. First of all, I also managed to throw in some other fine adjustments that will allow us to sort of hover over the ground and actually maneuver slightly forward and backwards, so we can plan where to place the DM safely, and where you and I will go before setting down." He pointed to a small joystick freshly installed on the panel in front of him. "During this period, we will be invisible to anyone in the immediate vicinity. After we decide where we want to put the DM, I'll keep the DM in this hover position, and it - and us - will remain invisible, as long as it keeps running in that mode. Here's the kicker: It is really important to remember that the very instant we step out off the DM and onto the ground, we will become visible. Not only that, but the machine will be invisible to us. Are you O.K. with that ?"

"Absolutely cool. I understand perfectly. Let's go. I am *so* ready!"

"O.K. San Francisco, here we come!"

He pushed the TRAVEL button.

The whirring of the Discovery Machine seemed to have yet another tone to it, an even different one from the others. Maria was beginning to notice the change in this sound, and to her it seemed like it was becoming more and more like a voice. A very deep and haunting voice. The thought sent a brief chill down her spine. She glanced at Phillip to see if he was feeling the same thing. But he was staring intently into the dials and watching the movement of the gear mechanisms.

As the machine began to wind down, they found themselves hovering a few feet over a cobbled road near a waterfront, or perhaps a bay, on the edge of what appeared to be a bustling young village, busy with people riding on wagons and horses and walking on sidewalks. Phillip moved the controls slightly and the DM moved out of the way and off the road to a flat area about 50 or 60 yards away from the village and nearer the water. He then slowly moved the machine behind a large wooden shed out of sight from the road.

"How about here, Maria? Think this will work?"

They looked around carefully. Maria said quietly, "Well, it doesn't look like anyone uses this area. I don't see anybody around. Probably as safe as anywhere could be." She patted the edge of the machine. "Phillip, your control changes for the machine are awesome. We can maneuver this like a car!"

Phillip was concentrating. "O.k. I'm going to lock the controls in the hover position. Let's take a good look at this location before we leave the area, because we won't be able to see the machine once we step off. We'll even have to feel our way back aboard when it's time to leave."

"I'm set. Let's go."

They moved to the edge of the platform, looked around carefully to make sure no one was in sight, and stepped off onto the ground.

They found themselves instantly alone on the ground behind the shed, and the Discovery Machine nowhere in sight.

"Wow, this is weird," Maria said. "Are you sure the DM is still here, Phillip?"

"It sure better be. Let's see."

He bent down and moved his hand slowly toward where he thought the DM was located until his hand magically disappeared in front of his eyes. "Incredible!" He pulled his hand back quickly and examined it. "I could feel the edge of the platform! Try it!"

Maria bent down and slowly moved her hand forward to the same area and it too disappeared. She kept her hand out, obviously savoring the moment. "That is so incredibly cool!" She pulled her hand away and looked at Phillip with wide eyes brimming with excitement. "Phillip, we are going to have *so* much fun with this. Nobody is *ever* going to believe any of this."

"Do you care?"

"Absolutely not!"

"Me neither. Well, let's go find Levi Strauss and see what he's up to."

But something about leaving the Discovery Machine invisible implanted a feeling of uneasiness and fear in their hearts, a feeling they both intuitively shared without having to vocalize it. They both glanced back over their shoulders as they walked away, looking at where they left the machine. They moved out from behind the shed, and up onto to the road, and started following it up into the village up ahead of them, some two hundred yards away.

They stepped onto the first street, and were taken by the feeling of extraordinary activity and a feeling of everything being temporary. Although there were many wooden buildings on the street, on most of the buildings and storefronts, others were built of simple wooden frames supporting canvas covers. There was a three-foot-wide rickety wooden walk on both sides of the street that ran in front and joined to the buildings and tents. The street itself was a mixture of stones and rocks and dirt, pressed tightly together and very uneven. Heavy ruts from recent rains cut like deep veins across it, and passing wagons bounced roughly as they passed over on their way to their destinations, their passengers holding on to the wagon supports tightly to keep from getting bounced out onto the ground.

Many of the buildings had wooden false fronts, and some of the business establishments had roughly hand-painted signs displaying what was for sale within. As Phillip and Maria walked along the boardwalk, they noticed the names of these places, which included several saloons, an ore assay office, a hardware store (or tent in this case), and a large open yard surrounded by canvas, with a sign over the entrance that said,

Joseph's Café and Dining Hall

in large crude letters painted onto a piece of wood. They peeked inside and saw a couple of dozen men seated on bales of hay in the open, eating off plates balanced on their laps. There were also men seated at rough tables on uneven wooden platforms eating, and there was a line of men moving slowly past containers of food, where they were being served portions of food by people behind the containers. A man stood at the end of the line collecting money, and above him was a sign that read,

Eggs, $4.50 each

Maria looked at Phillip in amazement.

"Wow! And this is 1850! That is what is called *inflation!*"

"I'll say!" It's more like *extortion.*"

They moved back out on the boardwalk and continued on down the street, observing the traffic and the people. At the corner they saw a sign announcing that they were on Sacramento Street. They stopped in front of a livery stable. Maria was craning her neck all around, looking up and down the street.

"How do you think we'll spot Levi Strauss?"

"I don't know. Maybe he'll have some type of sign on his wagon. He *is* a merchant, so maybe he uses his wagon to advertise."

They watched every wagon that went by for almost an hour, but the ones they saw all had drivers much older than twenty years old behind the reins. Tired of standing, they sat on the edge of the boardwalk facing the street.

The very moment they sat down, a covered wagon with a dark blue canvas top pulled onto the street from a side street and continued in their direction. As it drew nearer, they could start to make out lettering on the canvas cover of the wagon. Clearly emblazoned on the dark blue canvas, in deep reddish-orange letters about six inches high were embroidered the words,

Levi Strauss Dry Goods.

A young bearded man, a little husky in build, sat on the buckboard seat holding the reins to his horse loosely in his hands. He glanced over toward Phillip and Maria and smiled.

Maria impulsively smiled and waved back. The young man touched the brim of his hat in greeting.

The two were on their feet, and as the wagon passed them, they stepped in back of it and fell into the pace of the wagon, following it closely. After about two blocks, the wagon turned into a side street and stopped on the corner beside a store front building with the same sign, only larger, neatly painted across the front of the wooden framed opening,

Levi Strauss Dry Goods.

Phillip and Maria walked to the front of the wagon and up alongside the driver's seat. The man looked down at them and smiled.

"Hi, kids. What's going on with you two?"

Maria was excited, but she hid it well. She asked calmly, with a charming smile on her face, "Hi. Are you Mr. Levi Strauss?"

"Yes, I guess I am. You can call me Levi. And who are you two? I don't remember seeing either of you around here before. In fact, we seldom see *any* children around these parts."

"Oh. Uh, I'm Maria, and this is Phillip. Uh, we're not from around here. Just visiting." She felt awkward.

Phillip interrupted, and he was nervous. "Yeah, uh, we just saw you come in and we were wondering what your dry goods business is all about. I mean, this is a busy Gold Rush town, and all, and I mean, uh, we're just curious about what you, uh, sell, here."

Levi laughed, and jumped down from the wagon seat. He walked to the rear of the wagon where he pulled back a flap. He then reached inside and pulled out a large bag and put it over his shoulder.

"Well, I guess I sell a little of everything. Why don't you both come inside and I'll show you around. Might even dig up some cookies or candy if you'd be interested."

Phillip and Maria smiled at each other.

"We'd like that," Phillip said.

Levi pulled a long black skeleton key out of his trousers, unlocked the door, and pushed it open, gesturing for them to walk inside. Inside, he set the bag on the floor and then reached inside another pocket and pulled out some wooden matches, and turned to an oil lamp that was sitting on a stool just inside the door. He lifted the glass, rolled the wick out slightly, struck a match with a long stroke against his trousers, and lit the wick. He lowered the glass and set the now rapidly brightening lamp back on the stool. The room came to life.

As Levi moved around the room lighting more lamps, Phillip and Maria were exposed to a collection of hard goods and supplies that was surprising. There were shovels and axes and hammers and saws, and buckets of all sizes of nails. Different sizes of tin pails and metal tubs and other containers hung from the walls. Large wooden barrels and open shelves sat open side by side, displaying fabrics and cotton cloth, and even a hint of silk fabric. Sets of glass-covered counters lined one side of the room, and beneath the glass in the shelves were many smaller containers filled with hard candies and licorices. And over in one side of the room, occupying the entire wall, were large rolls of canvas in dark hues of black, blue, gray, and some in tan shades. The children's eyes focused on the canvas. They looked at each other and walked over to the rolls.

Levi Strauss turned to Phillip and Maria. "I brought all this from New York. My family has a dry goods company there. I heard about this Gold Rush, and I just imagined that a lot of men used to being able to get whatever they wanted in bigger cities would need a lot of things they probably couldn't find in a rough gold rush town like San Francisco. It was a big gamble for me. It took me months of preparation to get here, and then a long time for more of my supplies to arrive later. I found this community, and this store, and I set up business as soon as possible."

"How is it working out so far?" Phillip asked, holding a piece of heavy blue fabric in his hands, and showing it to Maria. Maria touched the fabric and looked up with a smile into Phillip's eyes.

"Well, to tell you the truth, I'm doing all right, but I really haven't made a big impression here. Don't get me wrong, I'm not complaining. I am covering my expenses, but I really want to do something big here, and it just hasn't happened yet."

"I bet it will!" Maria said enthusiastically.

Phillip glanced at Maria with soft caution in his eyes.

"Thanks for your vote of confidence, Maria. I'm a strong supporter of standing firm on your beliefs and dreams. And I intend to take advantage of every opportunity that might come my way, whether I expect it or not."

At that moment, a knock sounded at the door, and a middle-aged man stuck his head in the door.

"Howdy," the man drawled softly with a heavy southern accent. "I was just curious about what y'all are sellin' in here. You mind if I come in and look around?"

"Not at all," Levi said. "Come on in and make yourself at home."

The man removed his hat and thick blonde locks of hair uncurled and lay against his shoulder. He walked in the door. Despite his rough appearance, he moved with a certain confidence and grace of an educated man, probably from some southern state, and was perhaps even a Confederate Officer. He was dressed in clothes that showed the abuse of very hard work. His boots had broken and re-tied laces, and his shirt had holes in it. His brown cotton pants showed signs of being carefully hand-patched many times, and were threadbare in many places. He walked slowly around the room, examining the items before him like a child in a candy store.

He turned to Levi. He talked with a genuine gentleness in his voice. "I see you've gotta lot of merchandise here Sir, but what is it you really specialize in? What did y'all come out here with to sell the miners and people like me that you don't think we have?"

"That's a pretty direct question, sir. I appreciate it." Levi thought for a moment. He glanced over to his wall of canvas.

"Well, Sir, I guess what I really thought you folks needed out here that I had a lot of was *canvas*. I thought you would need it for tents, and buildings, and packaging, and whatever else that might be called for. But when I got out here, to my disappointment I found that there were already of lot of canvas suppliers here before me. So, I've been trying to supply other items to fill peoples' needs." He smiled. "Not too much success with doing that either. To be truthful, I haven't yet found an item to supply that has attracted much attention, other than common supplies."

The man had made his way over to the rolls of canvas, and he started feeling the fabric and moving it back and forth over his hands. He turned to Levi. "You know something? It's too bad you're using all this stuff to make tents. What we really need out here is pants. Nobody makes pants that last very long under these conditions."

Levi looked startled. "What did you just say?" His eyes had widened and he was instantly in tune with what the man was saying.

"I said, everybody needs pants out here and nobody makes 'em worth a dang. They don't last. Cotton pants just don't last long at all. The dirt and rocks tear 'em up fast."

Levi walked quickly over to where the man was standing by the rolls of canvas. He picked up a piece of the canvas and seemed to look at it in a new light. He studied it closely, bending and twisting the fabric as if seeing for the first time. A spark began to grow in his eyes, and held out a piece of the canvas to the man. "See this material? What would you think if *I* made *you* a pair of pants out of it?"

The man looked surprised and a little taken back, but his interest showed clearly. "You can make a pair of pants out of this canvas?"

"Yes. I can make a pair of pants out of this canvas. Would you try them out and wear them around while you work if I made you a pair? I wouldn't charge you for them. I would consider it a favor to me. A sort of *experiment*."

"You bet I would!"

The two men began talking about the pants, and pretty soon Levi had pulled out a measuring tape and began measuring the man's legs and waist, and writing numbers on a piece of paper. They were talking excitedly between them.

Phillip nudged Maria and whispered quietly in her ear,

"That's it. That's how it got started. I think we'd better go now and head back for home. We can find out how it developed later. What do you think?"

Maria was obviously taken up by what she had seen and clearly reluctant to leave the room. She crinkled up her face. "Phillip, I want to stay and watch more of this." She hesitated because she realized her voice sounded a little like a whine. A faint wisp of frustration showed over her face. "Hmmm. I guess you're right. This isn't something that is going to happen in a couple of hours, and we don't have the time to watch it develop. I guess we'd better get out of here and back to the DM."

Phillip walked over to the two men engrossed in measuring and talking about the pants. He softly touched Levi's sleeve. "Mr. Strauss. I mean, Levi. We have to go home. Thanks a lot for showing us around."

Levi looked down at Phillip and Maria somewhat distracted, but very kindly. He turned to them. "Listen kids, you are welcome in my store at any time. Please come back and see me whenever you like. I would really like to talk to you both more. There is something about you two kids that is very different." He paused and looked at them thoughtfully. "And – " with a smile in his eyes, he said, "- on your way out, why don't you reach in that cabinet and pick out a few pieces of candy."

They laughed and walked over to the counter, opened it up

and randomly chose several pieces of candy, closed the cabinet door, and walked to the door.

"Thanks, Mr. Strauss." Maria said. "And good luck with the pants. This may be just what you were looking for. Goodbye."

They waved and walked out the door to the boardwalk.

Outside, they faced each other on the boardwalk. Impulsively, Maria reached up and with both hands pulled Phillip's head down to where she could reach it, and kissed him on the cheek. He was surprised. The question mark on his face was as clear as if it were drawn there with a marking pen. "That," she said with her hands on her hips, "was for making that such a great experience."

Phillip blushed slightly and smiled. Maria continued on her train of thought. "I keep thinking about how much we as a culture seem to take products and inventions so much for granted. We tend to overlook the fact that a lot of original thought was used to come up with any new concept."

Phillip nodded. Maria talked and they began walking back down the street toward the DM.

"It's a real stretch, don't you think? Aren't you amazed at what kind of imagination it takes to instantly recognize the opportunity of making *pants* out of canvas instead of *tents*? That's a huge gap, right? Levi Strauss must have had a *lot* of things on his mind, including that of just worrying about survival. And in the midst of all these concerns, he was still able to openly consider an off-the-wall product idea, so completely different from that which he was pursuing."

Phillip nodded his head in agreement.

"Mind boggling," he said.

They were nearing the edge of the village and the area where they had come onto the street. They turned and looked back down the street at the village. It was late afternoon, but the street was still busy with people walking, riding horseback, and driving wagons.

The sounds of hammers pounding nails, and people working and talking together in the distance drifted through the air, and combined with the clatter of hooves and metal rimmed wheels on the street. It was noisy. But it was a noise that neither of them was used to. It lacked the sounds of motors, and electricity, and traffic, and all the sounds from a time in the future. The noises they heard were all man-made.

Phillip mused. "I wonder what it's like here at night. And what do you suppose the miners in the gold camps do after they stop working on their claims at the end of daylight. I mean, we know there a lot of saloons here, but I'd like to think they did things besides just drink and get drunk and fight. And from what we've just seen in Levi's shop, these men aren't all ruffians. I would bet there are a lot of people here from backgrounds with at least *some* culture."

"Well," Maria said while she pulled and twisted a few strands of hair with her hand, "From what I've read, the smaller saloons at least had lady singers who sang over big upright pianos, and entertained the miners while they played cards at the tables. The piano players were for the most part their orchestra."

"Yeah," Phillip said, "And since there weren't many women here at the time, I bet these singers were a welcome sight to lonesome men who spent all their time working in the gold fields."

"Yep", Maria said. "And I read that the larger saloons and halls built stages where theatrical plays and skits were performed. Eventually, as the gold camps started taming down and families began to arrive, the appreciation of theater itself influenced change in the buildings, or at least the barrooms."

"Not too many libraries and schools here at this time that I can see," Phillip observed. "Or churches for that matter. I guess the pursuit of education and religion was a pretty personal thing that you really had to want to do a lot." He looked around again. "Also, when you think about it, probably a luxury too."

"Right. Also," Maria added, "Don't forget that these men for the most part were either here as single adventurers and fortune hunters, or out here alone, having left their families behind until they could muster enough money to send for them. They were all here in hopes of making it big. And I don't think that this was a very safe environment in these early days anyway for women and children. Look around. Do you see any other kids our age? Or even older? There isn't even law enforcement here."

"It's just a lot of people caught up in the excitement and fever of striking the big one and getting rich," Phillip said. "When you think about it, there's probably not much difference in what they were trying to do here in this time and what others were trying to do with start-up companies in the Silicon Valley a few years ago in our time. Both of these business attempts were get-rich-quick gambles based upon a big dream of success. My dad always says everything is just perspective."

They were off the road, and approaching the waterfront and the shed behind it, where they hoped to find the Discovery Machine still waiting for them. They were now going to have to face a fear they both had been harboring since they first left the machine invisible.

"Well, here's the shed," Phillip said quietly, with a little apprehension edged in his voice. "I'm standing where I did when I last touched the machine." He looked at Maria's face and took her hand gently. "I guess there's only one way to find out if it's still there."

Maria placed her other hand over Phillip's. He gripped her hand firmly, let go, and then dropped to his haunches.

"O.K. Here goes." He reached out tentatively and slowly toward where he thought the DM rested. Maria took a deep breath, closed her eyes, and crossed her fingers on both hands.

Chapter Eight: The Solution

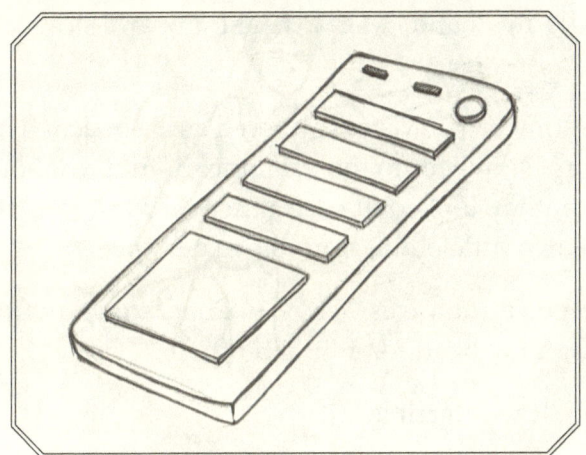

As Phillip inched his hand slowly toward where he thought the DM was, his mind was filled with thoughts of what would possibly happen if they couldn't find the Discovery Machine. They would be stuck in the year 1850, unable to ever return home to their own time period in the 2000s. He imagined how devastated their parents would be over their unexplained disappearance. He envisioned he and Maria orphaned and living alone in early San Francisco, and him trying to comfort her and stem the tide of tears that would flow from her eyes. That picture created such an intensely powerful pain and fear in Phillip's heart, that he had to forcibly eject it from his mind. He brought himself back to the task in front of him.

Just as he was beginning to feel the edge of panic approaching, the fingers of his hand suddenly disappeared, and he felt the platform of the DM. Phillip let out the enormous breath he had been holding. He could hear a huge sigh of relief from Maria.

"It's here," he said through a voice strained under the presence of worry.

"Thank goodness," Maria breathed.

He slowly climbed aboard, feeling his way, and immediately vanished from Maria's view. Like magic, Phillip's hand and arm extended out of the void in front of them, and Maria heard him say,

"Just take my hand, Maria. Come aboard slowly. I'll guide you."

"This is some trip," Maria muttered as she reached out. Phillip pulled her up slowly onto the machine. Both now aboard and on the platform, they looked at each other through eyes that were a little different, a little older, from the experience.

Maria's voice tone was heavy. "I had some awful thoughts going through my head for a little bit there."

"Me, too. It was terrible."

They sat back in their chairs exhausted, not moving or talking. With their heads back against the chairs, they watched seagulls glide in huge arcs above, the bright whiteness of their bodies in sharp contrast against the bright blue of the sky. They felt a brisk breeze from the bay roll over them and a slight mist in the air moistening their upturned faces. They could hear the sounds if the young city behind them, murmuring softly in its growth pains and excitement of newness.

After a while, Maria reached in the compartment where she had stowed the backpack and pulled it out. Without saying a word, she unscrewed the cap to the thermos and poured out a cup of hot chocolate. She took a brief sip, and passed it to Phillip. They sipped slowly, sharing the cup, savoring the pungent sweetness. The heat and immediate sweet taste of the hot chocolate on their taste buds was a brief but gentle shock of reality to both of them.

To be able to just sit and relax without fear was an indescribably delicious pleasure. They sat with the heads back against the chairs watching the scene of the early California bay area before them. The entire bay was filled with sailing ships of all sizes, coming in from the ocean, and leaving. And the scene of hundreds of tall-masted wooden sailing ships and boats moored to huge wooden piers along the bay edge, and the buildings that serviced them, was like stepping into some historical pictorial panorama stretched out before them. It was strange to not see the Golden Gate Bridge.

Finally, Phillip looked at his watch, and broke the silence. "That's the longest time yet we've spent on any of our trips. We'd probably better go home pretty soon."

"Yup," Maria said softly, in a more relaxed but very tired voice. "Let's go home."

Phillip leaned forward, checked the screen, set the controls, and pushed the RETURN button.

Over the increasing hum of the machine he said, "Here we go, Maria. See you there."

But Maria was already asleep.

It was about 4:30 when they arrived back in Phillip's workroom. He had to shake Maria awake gently.

"We're back, Maria", he said quietly. "And it's late."

Maria opened her eyes and slowly stood up from her seat.

"Come on", he said softly. "I'll help you down."

He stepped down and extended his hand up while Maria dropped to the floor. They covered the DM with its blanket, and walked down the stairs.

Phillip's mother was standing at the bottom with a surprised look on her face.

"Well, hello you two! I didn't think you were upstairs. I called quite a while ago, and even went up and looked in your room. I didn't see you, and I was beginning to get a little worried." She abruptly leaned forward and looked closely at Phillip's face.

"Phillip, how did you get that nasty cut on your face? Are you all right?"

"It's o.k., Mom," Phillip said cautiously. "I took a small tumble on the ground. It's nothing." He glanced sidewise at Maria. His mother touched the cut softly, and then noticed the tiredness on their faces. She continued with a slightly softer tone. "It's almost 5:00. And Maria, your mother called about an hour ago wanting to know if you were still over here."

"Sorry I didn't hear you when you came up. We were in my workroom with the door closed."

"That's o.k., honey. As long as you're both all right." She smiled. "Maria, we're only about an hour away from dinner. Would you like to stay and join us?"

"Thanks very much, Mrs. Prescott. But I think I'd better get on home, especially if my mother is worried about me."

"Any time you want, you know you're always welcome. I'll call your mother and tell her you're on your way home."

"Thanks, Mrs. Prescott."

Phillip walked her out to the porch. "Hey, Maria", he said softly. " Despite the fact we had a scare at the end, wasn't that a mind-blowing trip?"

"You bet. Totally cool." Maria said with a quick smile.

They stepped down to the sidewalk. Phillip said, "I've got an idea for fixing it so we won't have to do that scary search for the DM. I'll work on it and give you a call. Soon." He paused and looked closely into Maria's tired eyes. "Are you going to be all right?"

"I'm just fine, Phillip. And still excited. I know you'll fix it. You always do. Don't worry. Just call me." Maria walked away. She glanced over her shoulder and smiled back at Phillip.

He walked back into the house.

His mother was in the kitchen holding a small cantaloupe. She turned when he came in and walked over to give him an affectionate hug.

"Honey," she said, "I want to apologize for the time I've been having to spend away from the house, and you." She looked into his eyes for a moment and smiled. She walked back over to the sink, pulled a bowl out of the cupboard, and picked up a small knife. "This new job is really time-consuming. And I know it has really cut into the time you and I spend together." She began to carefully slice the melon in front of her and drop the slices in the bowl on the sink top. She handed him a piece, and gently touched his cheek with her hand. She smiled affectionately. "I know it's not easy for you. Your dad comes in late and tired every night from his job, and spends a lot of time in his workshop on his day off. It bothers me that you and I don't spend as much time together doing family things like we used to."

Phillip popped the melon piece in his mouth, picked up a chair, turned it around backwards, and sat down, chewing slowly, watching his mother continue dinner preparations.

"It's o.k. Mom. Besides, Maria and I have a lot of fun together." He added hastily, "And we do a lot of our homework together."

His mother turned from the sink and smiled. "I like Maria a lot, Phillip. She is obviously a very unusual girl." She looked at him over her shoulder with a teasing smile on her face. "I also think she has a little crush on you."

"Mom", Phillip said, a little flushed with embarrassment, "She's my best friend."

"I can see that. Tell me Phillip, aside from the obvious, that she is totally likeable and completely adorable, what do you like about her?"

"She's neat, Mom. She's also really smart, and I trust her completely."

A comfortable smile passed between them. Phillip set his chin on the top of the chair. She placed the bowl of melon slices on the table.

"Phillip, you know me. I'm really curious. Just what do you do together? Your teachers tell me you even spend most of your time together at school too."

Phillip stood up, turned the chair around, sat down, and leaned back tilting the chair slightly on its two back legs. "Just a lot of things, Mom. We've been together in school ever since I can remember. In fact I can't even remember not being with her. She makes me think, and be creative." He laughed and added, "She makes me laugh a lot too."

"That's important. Real important." She held a crouton from the salad she was fixing in front of his face until he opened his mouth and took it in. As he crunched on it she continued. "But what do you do together in your workroom all the time? Are you building something?" Her eyes took on a visible tease flavor. "Does it have anything to do with our missing T.V. sets, or those two red easy chairs that vanished mysteriously from the den?"

Phillip was beginning to feel a little uneasy with the direction of this conversation.

"Phillip, I have seen you drag bags and boxes upstairs almost endlessly, and my cousin Jim tells me that you are constantly in his back room at his electronics store rummaging through loose components and electronics parts." Her tone deepened a bit. "I told you I would always respect your privacy in that back work-room of yours, but I do have concerns for your safety. Are you doing anything that might accidentally hurt either you or Maria? Is there anything you want to tell me?"

Phillip squirmed a little in his chair. "That's a lot of questions, Mom. I promise you we're not doing anything wrong. We're being very careful."

"So you are building something."

"Uh, yes. We are, uh, experimenting with some stuff."

"Phillip, I trust you completely, and I know you're not doing anything wrong. But my curiosity is killing me. When are you going to share with me what you're doing? We used to share everything. I don't want to find out something after you or Maria have been injured. I would never forgive myself."

Phillip looked into his mother's eyes. She was intense. He thought about it. He and his mother had always been exceptionally close, as much sometimes as a pal as a parent. Because of his dad's job, they had always spent a lot of special time all of their own together. He realized suddenly he had never kept anything away from her, and had always shared with her all the things with which he had been involved. He knew her curiosity was genuine.

He decided. "O.K. Mom." He began cautiously. "Maria and I – "

The phone rang loudly. They both jumped, and the frustration on his mother's face from the interruption was plain. She tapped the table with her fingers. "Darn. I'm so sorry, Phillip. I have to answer this. I'm expecting a very important call about a listing for a huge estate, and it means the possibility of a huge commission. Please, can we finish this conversation later?"

He felt a wave of relief flow over him.

"Sure, Mom. I understand. It's o.k. Go ahead and take your call." Her hand was already on the receiver. She mouthed the words, "I love you," and said into the receiver,

"Hi, this is Maryanne. Oh, hi, Joyce. Thanks for your call."

Phillip pointed upstairs, and left the table as his mother continued her phone conversation. She blew him a kiss as he walked away.

Knowing he only had a little time before dinner would be ready, he went upstairs and into his workroom, where he stood looking at the covered DM. He pulled the blanket off and climbed up to his easy chair. He sat there in deep thought. His mother's comments had deepened his worries about the scare they had when they came back to the DM after the Levi Strauss trip. 'There has to be some simple way to make it easier and safer to find the DM when it is in its hover mode', he thought. He took out a piece of blank paper and started writing down what he knew about the situation. While he was thinking, he let his eyes wander around the room randomly. They suddenly came to stop and focused on a remote control from one of the T.V.s. It seemed to be shouting at him. He leaned slowly forward, focusing on it, and suddenly took a quick breath. "Of course!" he said out loud, as if he were talking to someone in the room. "I can program a remote to move the DM slightly forward out of its hover mode and become visible when we need to find it!. That's easy! All we will have to do is carry the remote with us. Maria will love this!"

Phillip was elated and relieved at the same time. He jumped down and ran over to the remote. Sitting at his desk, he opened the wand with a small screwdriver and peeked inside.

His mother's voice came up from downstairs.

"Dinner's ready, Phillip. Come on down."

Still elated, Phillip stood up, held the wand above his head in both hands, and did a little dance jig.

"Yes! Yes! Yes! Yes!" With each shouted 'yes', he stomped on the floor dancing. Then he set the wand back down on his desk, and watched it over his shoulder as he walked into the bathroom to wash his hands.

"I'm on my way, Mom," he shouted down the stairs, knowing he wouldn't be getting much sleep tonight. Phillip was stoked.

CHAPTER NINE: DARK CLOUDS

Phillip was still a little uneasy at dinner. He really had reservations about letting his mother in on everything that he and Maria had been doing. Especially if it meant telling her anything about the actual traveling through time on a time machine which, when he considered it, would probably be terrifying in his mother's eyes. In any perspective, it was indeed a monumental accomplishment and totally incredible.

He was also harboring a little guilt from his naiveté of not considering their safety more carefully on the first trips they took. He was still queasy in the bottom of his stomach thinking about losing contact with the DM. When his mother voiced her concerns over injury, and Maria's safety in the same breath, it was like someone had reached into his chest and given his heart a little punch. The thought of Maria being hurt was a terrible thought, and created an indescribable pain around his heart, and it made him abruptly grow up a bit and take a more careful look at what they were doing. He was beginning to feel enormous responsibility, and he wasn't sure he liked the feeling.

So, Phillip sat at the dinner table with his mother and father, talking small talk, and trying his best to keep the conversation centered on his mother's new potential Real Estate listing, and away from the subject of what was happening up in his workroom.

He knew his mother's routine at discussions, and instinctively knew at what point she would be considering turning the dinner conversation toward him. He kept alert, and as he felt that point started to arrive, he told a fib.

"Mom, I really hate to do this, but I have an online date in 10 minutes, to get some research info for our geography class. National Geographic. You know. So if you don't mind, I'd like to be excused to go up there." He paused for a reaction. "Upstairs. To get the information."

His mother's gaze was a little too penetrating and intense for his comfort. It was the same look she had on her face when they were talking about the workroom, and how she wanted to know what was happening. Her pause in answering was a little unnerving. She took a little sideways glance at her husband as if to see if he happened to be in tune with this conversation. This surprised Phillip, and he had the brief feeling that his mother was wanting to keep what had happened earlier between the two of them.

He glanced at his father, who appeared to be concentrating on the plate of food in front of him, and not looking to the right or left. Phillip realized his father hadn't said a word since he sat down at the table.

His mother looked back with what seemed to be a small touch of pain registering in her eyes. The intensity of her gaze had faded. After a few seconds, she quietly said,

"Sure, Phillip. That's o.k. Go ahead and do your thing. You and I can talk some other time."

Phillip stood up and took his plate over to the sink, feeling an odd tug on his heart as he did. "Thanks, Mom. I appreciate it." He glanced back at the table as he started up the stairs. His mother was quietly stirring some cream into her cup of coffee, and not looking up. As Phillip reached the top of the stairs, he realized that something wasn't right. It just didn't feel the same. His father was too quiet, and his mother's eyes were glimmering slightly, as if she were near tears.

He went up and sat down at his desk and pulled out a pen and piece of blank paper. He picked up the remote and popped it open, laying the two halves on his desk. He picked up the pen and clicked the point out. He sat there looking at the remote and the piece of blank paper. He clicked the pen closed. He clicked it open again. He felt like it was difficult to take a breath. He swiveled around in his chair and looked out the window.

The sky was turning darker with approaching nightfall, and shades of red and coral shafts of sunlight that splashed down from cracks in the clouds were being led into rapidly diminishing colors, eventually turning into light grays. He had always liked watching the changing of colors, and how the trees themselves changed in the dimming light. It always seemed to create a calming effect on him, although he had no idea why.

The pen felt heavy in his hand. He just couldn't put his finger on it. Whatever it was hung heavily in the atmosphere of the house like a cobweb of dark restricting bands across his chest. It sapped his energy and crushed the creativity and clear-thinking abilities that seemed to come so naturally to him.

Unable to focus, he set the pen down on his desk, stood up, and walked over to the stairs. He decided to talk with his mother, and started down the stairs. About halfway down, he stopped when he began picking up pieces of conversation between his mother and father. He didn't feel comfortable eavesdropping, but he didn't want to just barge in and interrupt them. So he just sat down on the stairs and listened. The stair squeaked softly.

"Oh, Vincent," his mother was saying, in a voice strained with emotion. "I just don't know how we can get through this. My job is really just starting, and I haven't made any commissions yet. I only have one listing in place, and almost everyone says it will be several months before I get any significant income. Losing your income will make things really hard for us right now. Is it definite?" Are you sure they're going to let you go?

"It's *not* definite." His father's voice was heavy and dark. "But they're planning on letting two more engineers from my department go. I *am* second in place with seniority, but I do worry that they might be trying to bring younger blood into the organization to save money on salaries and pension considerations."

"Do you have any back-up plan in place, or other ideas in case you do get fired?"

"Not really." He dropped his voice. "Maryanne, I hate this. The characteristics that exist in describing job losses in the Silicon Valley are volatile. My own company has cut back almost 20% of its personnel, and a lot of manufacturing and programming is now being outsourced to India, with what looks like more headed that direction." He paused and slowly closed and opened his eyes. "I don't know where the company is heading. And with the economy in the can, everything from housing costs to food is being affected. Everyone is sweating it. Even some of our VPs."

Phillip could see the back of his mother's head. She had her chin resting on her left hand, her elbow on the table. She was looking down at the table. There was a long, silent pause. "We just can't lose this house, Vincent." Her voice was so quiet Phillip could just barely make out her words. "It's all we have. We've been here since Phillip was born. This is the only home he has ever known. We just *can't* lose the house," she repeated.

"Maryanne." Phillip couldn't see his father, but he could hear the pain in his voice. "I'm doing everything I can possibly do." The silent pause was so great that Phillip could hear the faint sound of traffic down the street. "I promise I'll let you know about *anything* that happens."

"Oh, Vincent."

He had heard enough. He stood up quietly and climbed silently back up the stairs and into his room, leaving his door open. His heart was heavy as he sat at his desk and stared blankly at the remote in front of him.

After a while, he heard footsteps on the stairs and then his mother's voice.

"Hey, Phillip. Do you mind if I come in?'

"Sure, Mom. Come on in." He took a deep breath.

His mother came in the room. She was smiling, but the smile wasn't like any smile Phillip had ever seen before. He could feel sadness in her voice. She smiled again.

"It always amazes me at how neat your room is, Phillip." She walked slowly around the room, looking at different items he had accumulated, as if seeing them for the first time. "You've been an original from the very beginning, Phillip", she said, as she slowly circled the room. As she passed the door to his workroom, she paused and glanced at it briefly, and he could feel her curiosity swell. But she kept slowly working around the room. Finally, she came up behind him at his desk, put her hands on his shoulders, and bent down to plant a kiss on the top of his head. He reached his hand up and she took it and held it firmly.

"What's wrong, Mom?" He turned and looked up into his mother's eyes. They were brimming and glistening with the nearness of tears. She pulled up a chair and sat down facing him. She picked up his hand and held it in both of hers.

"Phillip," she began slowly. "I guess you've noticed that your dad has been very quiet lately. He's under a lot of stress because of his job. Well, there is a possibility that he may lose it, even after all these years of working for that company." She met Phillip's eyes with a penetrating gaze that went deeply within him. She smiled again, as if trying to send reassurance his way. "Phillip, I heard you on the stairs, so I know you overheard at least part of our conversation."

"I wasn't trying to be sneaky, Mom. I just didn't know what to do. I'm sorry."

"It's *all right*, honey. You have every right to know what is going on." She took a breath. "The truth is, we don't have *any* facts. Just speculation, based on what we've been observing that has been happening in the Silicon Valley for the past few years. It doesn't seem to be getting any better, and a lot of people are very nervous."

Phillip took a deep breath. "Will we have to move, Mom?'

"Honey, we are doing everything we can to stay here, and we hope we're a long ways from anything that drastic happening right now." She looked into his eyes deeply. She could see the confusion in his eyes. She also saw strength.

She had seen that strength many times while he was growing up, and experienced its uniqueness when she miscarried three years ago. It had been a late miscarriage, and they had already determined by ultrasound that it was to be a girl, a baby sister for Phillip. She and Phillip had spent many nights talking about his baby sister's arrival, and what it would be like to be a big brother. He was excited about the arrival.

Phillip had been at school when his mother was taken to the emergency room at the hospital. His father came by and took him out of class and brought him to the hospital. On the way, he had to break the news to Phillip about the loss of the baby. By the time they reached the hospital, Phillip was sitting motionless and very quiet in his seat. His father went in first and spent some time with is mother alone, and then he came out and brought Phillip in. He left the room so the two of them could be alone. Phillip walked slowly over to her bed. As he approached, a tear rolled untethered down his mother's face, leaving a damp trail behind it.

"Phillip, I am *so* sorry."

At that moment, Phillip did something that totally amazed and surprised her, and endeared himself deeply in her heart. He walked up and sat on the edge of her bed. Then he picked up her hand by the fingers, and touched his lips to the back of her hand, completing the gesture with no less grace and class than a European gentleman would have done. "It's O.K., Mom. As long as you're all right."

"Oh, Phillip." She pulled him close to her and held him tightly. They stayed in that embrace for a long time.

Vincent and Maryanne relived that incident with great fondness and pride over the years, wondering how a seven-year-old boy could possibly be that sensitive and worldly.

That memory surged back as she now sat beside him in his room, three years later, confronting yet another difficult task.

"You know, Phillip, from the beginning you have pretty much gone through your life on your own agenda. From a very young age you have chosen directions to go that felt best to you only. And we noticed that it seldom has bothered you that your friends at school either approved or disapproved the things in which you found interest. You've always been confident, and clear-headed in your thinking." She paused for a moment.

"And you know what? Your father and I have to come to depend on that level-headedness from you. I guess we depend on you a lot. And that's obviously why we trust you so much." She smiled and kissed him again on the cheek. "We'll make it through this, Phillip. Don't worry. Worry just gets in the way, don't you think? Worry uses a lot of energy, and we'll need all the positive energy we can muster to get through this strange deck of cards that life seems to deal us on a regular basis."

"Yeah, Mom. I agree. Maria says the same thing all the time. She keeps telling me to not 'sweat the small stuff'".

Maryanne laughed.

"Maria is a trip also. I suspect there's a lot going on in that cute head of hers." She put on a mock expression. "And that brings us back to our interrupted conversation." She pointed her finger at Phillip. "I believe you were just about to tell me what you two are cooking up."

Phillip swallowed. "Mom, I had already decided I was going to tell you about what we're doing. And I want you to know that I am doing everything I can to take *any* danger out of it. I *promise* you."

"Why do I get the feeling that this isn't just some complicated chemistry experiment?"

"Well, you're right, Mom. It's a little more than that. I was really hoping that Maria cold be here to talk about it with you too, because the original idea was hers. But I – "

Phillip's desk phone rang loudly. He glanced at the caller I.D. "It's Maria, Mom."

"Tell you what", his mother said. "Why don't you ask her to come over tomorrow morning and we can all sit down and talk about your project, or whatever it is you are working on."

Phillip didn't know if he felt relieved or not. "That's fine, Mom. I'll ask her to come over."

He picked up the phone and his mother walked out of the room and down the stairs.

"Hi, Maria," he said into the receiver. "Mom and I were just talking about you." He listened intently, tapping his fingers on the desk nervously. "Yeah. My mom likes you a lot. She says that you're cute, and adorable, and very smart." Talking to Maria was already making him feel better. He laughed. "Well, I'm glad you feel that way about her too. "Yes, I *do* feel lucky to have a mother like her. What are you doing right now? Uhuh. Uhuh. I agree. Yes, I did." It was hard to put a cap on Maria's enthusiasm when she was on a roll. "Yes. Uhuh." He waited for a break in her words. She finally took a breath and he jumped in.

"Maria. I do have news. Yes! All sorts of it. First, you are going to love this. I thought up a way to find the DM when we return to it, without just blind searching the area we left it in. It's so simple. I can't believe it's so simple.

"What?" He laughed at her interruption. "How? The *remote*. I can re-program the T.V. remote to move the DM slightly forward out of the hover mode and make it visible when we need it! Yes! Uhuh. That's right. All we have to do is to make sure we carry the remote with us at all times. Probably a good idea to keep extra batteries too. Pretty cool, huh? I can have it ready by tomorrow morning. Yeah." He took another deep breath as if he were going to swim underwater.

"And that brings up another little thing. It's about my mother. She, uh, uh, well, she has been really persistent about finding out what we're doing." He grimaced and held the phone away from his ear at her instant loud shouting, and looked at it. "It's O.K., Maria. It's O.K. *It's O.K.* Don't freak out. We'll have to eventually let them know what we're doing. What? No, I don't think we can hold off much longer. Yes. Yes. YES." He took another quick breath. "In fact, she asked me to have you over in the morning so we can all talk about it. Maria. I -, Maria -, Maria, calm down. It's *O.K., Maria.* Just relax. I promise it will work out. Now, can you come over tomorrow morning? Maybe you and I can get together first before we get my mother involved. No, I'm not just trying to sweet talk you. You can? Great! How about sometime between 9:00 and 9:30? Thanks, Maria. You're the best. You'll see. It will all work out great. I'll see you tomorrow morning."

He hung up the receiver and sat down. He felt like he had just wrestled a bear.

"Wow. I feel beat up", he said aloud. "A mad redhead and an overly curious mother. What am I getting myself into?"

He picked up the remote and began to focus on it. He soon lost track of time.

CHAPTER TEN: THE INITIATION

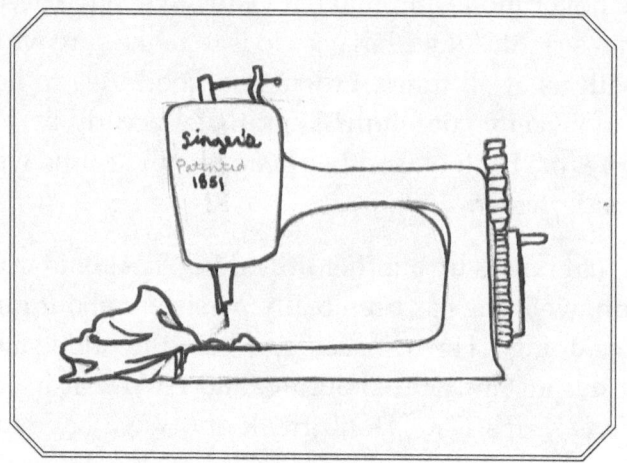

Phillip hadn't hit his bed until around 1:00 a.m., and had been up since 6:00. Now consumed with every detail of the machine's operation, he had removed the insides of the remote control and re-set them into a metal box about the same size, not wanting to take the chance that the plastic might break. He rewired it and included a sensor that could be the key to the communications line between the DM and the remote control, and tried it out at midnight. It was totally successful. He was tired, but he was ready.

At 9:15, he heard Maria at the front door and ran down the stairs to meet her. But his mother was already at the door.

"Hi, Maria," she said, with a genuine smile of welcome on her face. "Come on in. I'm so glad you're here. I am so eager to see what you two have been working on."

The expression on Maria's face was a plastic collage of smile and apprehension.

"Thanks, Mrs. Prescott." She looked past her to Phillip just coming up to the door behind his mother. "Hi, Phillip." Maria's eyes widened slightly. Even though she was smiling, Phillip knew her well enough to detect her attitude.

"Hi, Maria." He grimaced slightly behind his mother's turned head. Maria kept a stoic face.

"Is that a thermos in your hand, Maria?"

"Yes, Mrs. Prescott. Phillip and I seem to drink a lot of chocolate. We like it. It helps break up the day."

"I know the feeling," his mother said. "Hey, listen. You're father is conveniently out of town, so we've got the place to ourselves. I've still got about a half hour or so of chores to do down here. How about you both going upstairs and I'll come up when I'm finished. Is that all right?"

"Great, Mom. Just come on up when you want. We'll be up there."

His mother walked back into the kitchen and smiled as she watched them bounding up the stairs, trying to remember when she had that type of energy to spare.

Up in Phillips room, Maria was instantly eight inches from his face, in her 'don't mess-with-me'-hands-on-hips posture, and her eyes were flashing.

"Phillip, is your brain pure mush!? *How* are we *possibly* going to explain this to your mother? She will freak out."

"Maria," he said, as calmly as he could. Phillip knew Maria very well, and he knew the only way to keep her calm was to *talk* and *act* calmly. "Please trust me. I know my mother. She and I have been through a lot together. She *will* handle this, and maybe even surprise us. Let's just take it slowly, and give her a chance. O.k.? Besides, let me remind you: *You* didn't freak out when I showed *you* the DM."

Maria studied his eyes as if she were trying to pick microscopic pieces of lint from them. "All right, Phillip. The ball's in your court. I hope we don't screw this up. We can get in a lot of trouble."

"We'll be *fine*, but I will need your help, too. Just be yourself. You're terrific, and Mom likes and trusts you."

"That's one of the things I'm afraid of. *Losing* that."

"That won't happen."

"I'll hold you to that, mister." She paused, still holding him in her gaze like a piece of meat on a shishkabob. "Now," a subtle soft shift in her concentration was visible on her face. She smiled slightly. "I *have* to tell you what I researched on Levi Strauss."

"Great! Great! Let's hear it." He sighed deeply in relief to get off the subject and away from her piercing eyes.

"According to what I read, the word spread around fast about Mr. Strauss' pants in the community. By the way, he named them, 'Coveralls.' They were actually pants with long straps on them to go over the shoulders. Levi Strauss *did* alter the material slightly after some of the miners mentioned that although they loved the strength and durability of the pants, the stiffness of the material tended to chafe their legs. So Levi Strauss had a softer material imported in, essentially the stuff similar to what is used now. The material was perfect. Everybody loved the pants, and Levi Strauss increased production of the pants as fast as he could. The only large problem seemed to be in keeping up with the demand. He kept building larger and larger facilities and employing more people to work in his plant. He was a natural businessman. Did you know that some of those same pants, well over *150 years old,* are still in existence today? Now *that's* really saying something!"

"Wow," Phillip mused. "That's a great story. Really nice research. You know, Maria, you're going to really go somewhere. Now, *where,* I don't know."

She elbowed him in the ribs.

"O.k. Now let me show *you* what I've done with this remote, so we'll both know how to work it if we have to." He picked up the steel rectangular box and held it out to Maria. She examined it closely, turning it over and over. "Phillip," she said, with delight written across her face, "This doesn't look at all like that black plastic remote. This looks more like a piece of X-Ray equipment, especially with this infra-red LED. It's cool. Does it work?"

"Like a charm. Do you know what this means, Maria? It means we can leave the DM in its invisible hover mode, and when we want to find it, all we have to do is to slowly move this fader switch to bring the DM slowly into focus so we can see it. No worries, no fears. We can concentrate totally on our explorations and be confident of our way home being secure. Now, is *that* not cool?"

"Totally." She looked at him with a new softness in her eyes, and touched his hand lightly. "Phillip, I have to say something, and don't get all big-headed about this. I know I give you a lot of static all the time, but you had better be around when I grow up and eventually want to get married. I think I would kill any girl that thinks she can get her hooks into you."

Her comment caught Phillip off guard, and his face turned a brilliant red. But as he thought about it, he couldn't imagine not having Maria in his life.

Before he could develop that thought any further, his mother called from the stairs.

"Hey, you guys. Can I come in?"

"Come on in, Mom."

Maryanne came in and looked around the room, breathing a little hard. "You know, I don't know how you can run up and down these stairs all the time. I'm out of breath just climbing them once." She came over and sat down beside them. "Well, Maria, you two must really get along well. You spend a lot of time together."

"Phillip is my best friend, Mrs. Prescott. Your son is a really cool guy, and I love being with him."

Maryanne laughed with pleasure over Maria's straight-from-the-hip directness.

"You know what, Maria? *You* are a totally cool young woman." She looked at them both and smiled. "All right. *What* are you into up here? *What* have you been doing that is so secretive?"

Phillip and Maria exchanged glances. "O.K., Mom. We are going to show and tell you everything. But we need your promise that you won't freak out over what you are going to hear, *and* see."

Maryanne hadn't missed the visual exchange between the two children. She sensed something important was before her. "Phillip, I can only promise you that I will be as open-minded as possible. If I feel that there is danger involved, I'll have to use my judgment. Is that O.K.?"

Phillip and Maria exchanged another glance. Maria nodded slightly to Phillip.

"Mom, you and I have been through a lot together. I believe you can handle this."

"Phillip, whether you realize it or not, I'm actually a big girl now. Your mother, yes, but I can *handle* anything."

"O.K., Mom. Here we go." He took a short breath. "A while back, Maria and I were looking through pictures and wondering about where and how certain discoveries and inventions came about. Maria stated that it would be neat to actually see how these discoveries were made."

"What do you mean?"

"I mean, it was her idea to, well, actually *visit* the time period and location where the discovery took place."

"But Phillip, that would mean going back in time." Maryanne smiled, and then gasped audibly as she realized what she had just said. "Are you trying to tell me that you are trying to put together a machine to take you back in time? A *time* machine?"

"Yes, Mom. That's it exactly. Well, that's not what *we* call it, but I guess that's actually what it is. A time machine."

Maryanne looked at Maria.

"Is this true? Is this true, Maria? Is this what you two are trying to build?"

"Well . . . " Maria glanced uneasily at Phillip. "Yes, Mrs. Prescott."

Phillip looked at Maria, then back at his mother. "Mom, Maria is trying to tell you that we are not *trying* to build the machine."

"What do you mean?"

"I mean we're not *trying* to build it." He paused apprehensively. "I mean we already *have* built it."

Maryanne's face went pale.

"Phillip, this is a reach if this is a joke. This is scary stuff."

"Mom, it's no joke. We really have built this machine. It's in my workroom. Right in there." He pointed. Now, Mom, here's the point where I'm really concerned about you. So please steel yourself."

"No, Phillip." Maryanne was visibly shaken. "You're not going to tell me – "

"Yes, Mom, I am. We have already tried it out. We have already gone and come back several times. We have actually traveled back to other times. It works."

"Hold on, you guys. This is a bit much for me. My heart is beating very hard right now. I just can't believe this. This is Science-Fiction, and *trite* Science-Fiction at that."

Phillip thought for a moment. He had an idea. "Mom, do you

remember that candy you commented about? Remember, you said it looked like 'antique' candy from another time? Well, it was. Maria and I were given that candy by a famous merchant in 1853 during the Gold Rush."

Maryanne was incredulous. "You were given that candy in the year 1853? Someone gave you that candy in the year 1853? You went back to the year 1853 in this machine that you built? Phillip, I'm having a hard time here. Help me out."

Maria joined in with her trade-marked intensity. "It's true, Mrs. Prescott. Everything Phillip has said is true. We've visited wonderful places, and have had incredible experiences. We've learned *so much!*"

Maryanne's hands were white-knuckling the arms of her chair.

"O.K.", she said through gritted teeth. "I did promise to keep an open mind. So I guess you'll have to show me."

To her surprise, Maria extended her hand out to her.

"Come on, Mrs. Prescott. Let me show you Phillip's machine."

They walked to the door of the workroom. Phillip walked over to the wall light switch and flicked it on.

"This is where it happens, Mom. Come on in."

Maria led Maryanne through the door by her hand. The machine was covered by the blanket. It stood ominously before them. A lamp was on behind it, and the shadows from its form were casting dramatically onto the walls of the room, like a scene from an old monster movie.

"Are you ready?" Phillip asked.

"As ready as I'll ever be, that is if I'm not already crazy, or dreaming."

Phillip and Maria went to opposite sides of the covered machine, gripped the edges of the blanket, and quickly pulled it off.

Maryanne rolled back on her heels at the sight of the apparition before her.

Maria jumped aboard and Phillip followed. Phillip turned around and held out his hand to his mother.

"Come on aboard, Mom. How would you like to meet Levi Strauss in person?"

CHAPTER ELEVEN: A NEW PERSPECTIVE

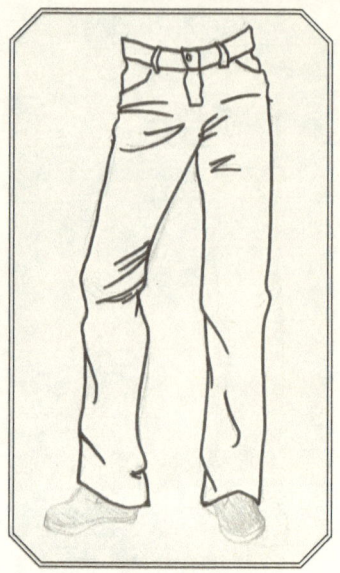

Maryanne climbed aboard the DM with Phillip's help. He motioned for her to sit in his chair.

"Well, here you are, Mom. We call this the Discovery Machine".

"Well, well, well." Maryanne sat in the red chair studying the machinery and layout in front of her. "*Well*, here we are." she said again. "Wow. I'm still a little shaky, but I've got to admit, this is pretty unique." She leaned forward and looked more closely at the array before her. "Hmmm. That video screen there looks very familiar. It looks surprisingly similar to my little personal Sony that mysteriously disappeared out of my study three weeks ago."

"Hmmm. Imagine that," Phillip said with a touch of mischief on his face. "What a odd coincidence."

"O.k.," Maryanne said with a little relief reflected in her voice. "I'm here. Tell me what this is all about."

"O.k., Mom. Here's our concept. The whole goal of putting a machine together was to enable us to visit a specific time and location, centered around a specific discovery or invention. There are some pretty neat electronics in this, Mom, although I have to admit I'm not sure yet how the internal search engines specifically determine what and where to go to match a search topic. I think I accidentally hit on something that works. If it will make you feel better, we have worked out a few bugs, and I figure we're about as safe as we can get right now."

"I'm not sure I want to hear a lot of detail about those 'bugs', and what happened," Maryanne observed. "Well, what do we do now? Are you going to show me how it works? And what was that you said about meeting Levi Strauss? Why Levi Strauss?"

"Maria," Phillip said, "What do you think about going back to see how Mr. Strauss has done since we last saw him?"

"It would be fun to set the arrival time for a year *after* our first visit. He should be in full swing by then."

"Good idea. Sounds good. Mom, I'm going to get you a jacket. Think you can snag the thermos, Maria?" He smiled at his mother, who had a very strange look bravely pasted on her face. "Why don't you look over the machine? Just don't touch."

Maria was already on her way off the DM and headed for Phillip's desk.

When Phillip came back up with his mother's jacket, Maryanne asked, "Phillip. Is that my old hand-held hair dryer mounted on your console? It's O.K. I don't care if it is, but what are you using it for?"

Phillip touched the motor mechanism of the old dryer. "I took the heating element out. The fan makes a great little cooling unit for my internal electronics that tend to get a little warm."

Maria was already back with the thermos.

"Now. Mom. Unlike the Science-Fiction Time Machines you

see in movies that stay in one location, and time passes forward or backward around them, our machine is an actual traveling craft with movement flexibility built in. Although we will always return exactly to this place, we can go anywhere and move in any direction, as well as actually fly." Phillip put his hand gently on his mother's wrist. "Since we only have two chairs on the DM, Maria and I will share this one to be close to the controls, so you'll have to move to Maria's chair."

Maryanne stood up and moved over to the other chair.

"Nice chairs, by the way." She raised her eyebrows.

Maria had been writing on her pad. She turned to Phillip and handed him her notes. "Phillip, here are your guidance points to get us back to San Francisco one year later than when we were there before. We should arrive at about the same spot in the area by that shed as before."

"*Whoa*, guys," Maryanne said nervously. "Did you say San Francisco? Are we actually going to go *now*? I mean, is this it? Right now? Is it safe? Will we get back O.K.?"

"That's exactly what Maria asked the first time we went," Phillip said. "And we made it back. Just try to relax and enjoy this. It will be an experience completely different from what you have *ever* done before."

"*That* is what I'm afraid of."

"It's amazing and fun, Mrs. Prescott," Maria said. "I promise you will enjoy it very much."

"It's time," Phillip announced. "Are we set?"

"Oh, you guys," Maryanne almost whimpered, "This is scary."

Phillip leaned forward and typed in the coordinates and the words,

```
San Francisco, California, 1854
```

He placed his finger on the TRAVEL button. "O.k. Here we go." He pushed the button.

Maryanne held on tightly to the arms of her chair as the humming and vibrations of the machine increased.

As things eased into focus around them, they found themselves hovering just off the ground, near the location they had been before at the waterfront. They could hear the traffic of wagons and horses nearby in the village. It was a clear day. A brisk breeze was blowing, and they found themselves slowly starting to drift. Things seemed the same, although Phillip and Maria were surprised to see a carriage approaching in the open space near the shed. On the buckboard seat sat a man with the reins in his hand, and a woman beside him, and peeking out from behind them in the wagon was a young boy. Their drift was taking them into the path of the carriage.

"Phillip," his mother whispered. "That wagon is going to hit us."

"I'll fix that." Phillip moved the joystick slightly and they floated away from the carriage and over to behind the shed, where he stopped and locked the DM into its hover mode.

Maryanne's eyes were wide open. "Phillip," she said. "The people on that wagon. They were close to us. They didn't even seem to notice us."

"That's because we're invisible, Mrs. Prescott," Maria said. "We're not in focus to them, so they can't see us. And we'll stay invisible as long as we remain on this platform. The second we step off anyone can see us."

"Wow," was all Maryanne could say. She muttered softly to herself and rubbed her arm, "Am I awake?"

"Maria," Phillip said. "We'll have to tie the DM to an anchor. Did you notice how the wind blew us?"

"Yup, I noticed. If we hadn't solved the remote control problem, we might have had a *real* hard time finding the DM again. I saw some nylon chord and a piece of steel rod in the storage locker. We can drive the rod into the ground and tie the DM to it."

"That'll work."

Maria opened the locker and retrieved the chord and rod. Phillip reached for them and suddenly noticed what his mother was wearing. "Maria, look at Mom's pants."

Maryanne was startled. "*What?* What *about* my pants?"

"Omigosh" Maria said. "They're *jeans.*" She looked closer. "They're even *Levis.*"

"Well, of course they're Levis. They're my 501's. That's all I wear around the house. What's the deal? What's wrong with them?"

"It's probably going to be just fine, Mrs. Prescott," Maria said reassuringly. "It's just that we are taking you to meet the man who designed and manufactured those pants you are wearing. The thing is, those 501's you are wearing were manufactured some 150 years *after* he designed them. He may find that a bit curious, if he sees them."

"Oh." Maryanne touched her pants, seeing them differently for the first time.

Maria had been checking out the surrounding area. "It looks like it's clear enough to step down," she said. "Let's anchor the DM. Also, it doesn't look like we'll need our jackets. It's pretty warm."

Maryanne turned to Maria. "Are we really in the year 1854, Maria? Those wagons looked authentic."

"Let me check, Mrs. Prescott." She glanced at the screen and pushed a small button Phillip had just installed. The screen printed out,

Year 1854, San Francisco, California, confirmed.

"Yup. We're here."

Phillip jumped down from the platform.

"O.K., Maria. Hand me that rod. I think there's a hammer in that locker, too."

"Already got it." She handed the rod and the hammer down to Phillip.

He moved to the rear of the platform and pounded the rod firmly into a crevice in under the shed.

"O.K. Now hand me the cord."

He handed her back the hammer and took a piece of cord from her and looped it around one of the back support beams of the DM. He then tied it to the rod and knotted it tightly.

"Done. What do you say we get going?"

Maria jumped down and they both turned to help Maryanne off the DM. When she stepped down, she turned around to find the machine missing.

"What – !?"

"It's still there, Mrs. Prescott," Maria said. "And it will be there when we get back. Phillip has the remote with him."

They walked over to the road and started toward town. Phillip said, "When we first arrived here a year ago in *this* time, there weren't many women or families here. Just *men* trying to find gold. So it's pretty interesting to see a carriage with a man and his wife and child in town. There's obviously been some real progress here since we visited."

As they approached the village, they could see that most of the canvas type buildings had been replaced with permanent wood framed buildings. The village looked more like a real community, and the feeling of being temporary had almost disappeared.

"A lot of those buildings were tents made out of canvas the last time we were here, Mrs. Prescott," Maria explained. "It looks more like a real town now."

Maryanne was intently taking in all that was happening around her.

"Check out those clothes, you guys," she said, pointing to some people leaving a hardware store. "This is amazing. I just can't believe this is happening."

"You'll get used to it soon, Mom." Phillip smiled at his mother.

"Hey, Phillip," Maria said. Levi's shop is on this next block isn't it?"

"I think so."

As they walked along the boardwalk, Maryanne studied every building front they passed. "This is unbelievable."

"Actually, Mom," Phillip said. "This is quite a bit different than some of the places we have been." He and Maria exchanged glances.

"O.K.," Maria said. "This is the street. I remember it because it was across the street from that Livery Stable."

They walked to where Levi Strauss' shop had been.

"Here it is," Phillip said. The store was closed. Maria walked to the door.

"Here's a sign. Look, Phillip. It says he's moved." She read it out loud.

Levi Strauss has moved to
90 Sacramento Street,
and is open for business.
Levi Strauss, Proprietor

They walked back out to the street on which they had been walking.

"This is Sacramento Street," Maria said. "I guess that means Mr. Strauss is that way," she pointed.

"Guess so. Let's go."

They continued walking down Sacramento Street. A lot of changes were evident, especially in the storefronts. Very few hand-scribbled signs were visible, having been replaced with more professionally done commercial signs, as well as nicely painted window layouts.

"Just *look* at this store," Maryanne said as they approached a picturesque grocery and dry goods store. Can we go in for just a minute?" She was excited.

"Sure, Mom," Phillip said. "Mom, I think I'd better remind you. Don't try to buy anything. We don't have currency of the period."

"That's o.k.," she said. "I just want to look. Oh, wow," Maryanne exclaimed as they stepped inside the store. "Can you believe this?"

Everything they had ever read about from stores of this period was there. Pickle barrels with ladles attached. A pot-bellied wood-burning stove sat in the middle of the store with chairs placed around it. Cupboards full of every type of pot or pan imaginable. Large sacks of flour, beans, sugar and salt sat on the floor. Lanterns and oil lamps were everywhere hanging from the ceiling and walls. Rows of apothecary jars in a myriad of colors from their contents, filled with every type of confection, or pasta, or spice available, lined the shelves behind the counter. In the back part of the large room were bolts and bolts of cloth in different patterns, and sitting in the front of the material was a small, shiny, black sewing machine on a display pedestal.

Maryanne stopped abruptly in front of the machine and

gasped audibly. "Oh, Phillip. Look at this old Singer!" She moved close to examine it. "It's fantastic!"

"Mom, I think I'd better remind you. That is not an old Singer. It's brand new. At least it is in this time."

"Yes, I guess you're right, honey." She touched the machine. "What I would give to have this. I've always wanted an antique Singer."

"Hello, Ma'mm." A slender man with gray and balding hair, wearing a white apron over his overalls, walked up at that moment. "Welcome to my store, and San Francisco . You folks must be new in town."

"Thank you," Maryanne said. "Yes, I guess you might say we're new here." She turned to the sewing machine. "What a lovely Singer you have here. It's beautiful."

"Yes, ma'mm. It's the top of the Singer line and brand new. It's pricey, but you can't get any machine like this better. Would you like to try it out?"

"Oh!" Maryanne exclaimed. "I would be afraid to try, but could you show me how it works?"

"I'd love to, Ma'mm." The clerk smiled and sat down on a stool in front of the machine. He pointed. "These spools here hold your thread, and you put them into this needle that goes up and down over this little box. The needle is powered by this treadle board down below. You just move your foot up and down to make it run. It not only advances the material on the top of this flat area here on top, but helps to keep running thread through the needle from the spool on the top of the machine. Simply take two pieces of material you want to join together – ," he picked up two pieces of scrap material, "- and place them right next to this needle. Pull up the little lever and move the material under the needle like this. When you get the needle placed where you want it above the material, push the lever down to the material and turn this big wheel on the top of the machine. Once it gets moving, start your treadmill going. The machine will do the rest. All you have to do is guide the material. You can go as fast or as slow as you want, depending on how fast you move your feet."

"That's wonderful," Maryanne said. She looked at Phillip, and then Maria. "Do you mind telling me how much you are asking for it?"

"Well," the clerk said, "As I mentioned, this new Singer *is* a little pricey. I'm asking forty-five dollars for it."

"Forty-five dollars!?" She was aghast.

"Yes, I know that seems a bit much,'" he said apologetically. "How about if I brought it down to a flat forty-two?"

"I – " Maryanne was perplexed. She looked around and took in where she was and looked at Maria. "Oh, I wish I could. I really wish I could. In another time I would love to have it. I'm sorry. Thank you so much for showing it to me. It's quite beautiful."

"Well, ma'mm, it'll be here until it gets sold. You're welcome to come back anytime. Anytime at all."

"Thank you," Maryanne said. She touched the Singer. Then she turned back to Phillip and Maria. "Well, you two. I guess we'd better go."

Outside the store, Maryanne said, "I'm sorry, guys. I probably violated some rule of yours in there. That was wonderful. Phillip, do you have any idea how much I loved seeing that Singer, and that wonderful store? Thank you so much. Both of you." She pulled them to her and hugged them.

"You didn't break any rules. There aren't any. And you did great. There's more, Mom. There's going to be a *lot* more. Phillip squeezed his mother's hand.

"O.k." Maria said. Mr. Strauss' store must be very close. Let's keep walking. I just have a feeling we're all due for a big surprise."

CHAPTER TWELVE: BUSTED

Phillip and Maria were enjoying watching Maryanne's reaction to the young city of San Francisco, and the event of her traveling for the first time on the Discovery Machine. As they continued walking down Sacramento Street, she stopped in front of every storefront, and then would only reluctantly move on to the next.

The street climbed slightly, and when they reached the top of the hill, they stopped in amazement. Before them, on the right side of the street, was a very large building that was bustling with people going in and out of its large double doors. The building had a large false front, typical of the architectural design of San Francisco business buildings of the period. Across the white face of the building, in large two-foot-high block letters cut neatly from wood and boldly painted, were the words,

LEVI STRAUSS

"Would you look at that!" Phillip exclaimed. "Looks like Mr. Strauss has gone big time."

They waited at the door briefly while several customers left and cleared the way, then walked inside. They were immediately surprised at the vast size of the building. A good part of the interior held dry goods merchandise similar to the way it was displayed in Levi Strauss' old store, but the most obvious difference was in the vast size of the building, with bins after bins of clothes, displayed not unlike that of merchandising techniques used by major merchandisers in the 2000's.

Levi overalls dominated the merchandise in the front of the store, and these pants were arranged neatly by size. A sign on the front of the pants bins read,

Levi's Waist Overalls

Other bins held shirts and jackets of different materials as well as the material used in the Levis. There were at least twenty customers in the store shopping. Two very friendly lady clerks wearing long aprons over ankle length dresses were busy going from customer to customer, helping in size selection and answering questions. A low hum of excitement pervaded the atmosphere of the room, and a short line of customers waited patiently at the register to purchase their items. It was a very busy and dynamic store.

"This is pretty impressive," Maria said. She turned to Maryanne. "Mr. Strauss was the only one in the store the last time, Mrs. Prescott. Now look at it."

"I don't see Mr. Strauss anywhere", Phillip said, looking around.

"Let's ask at the register," Maria replied. They walked over to the woman at the counter and stood there until she noticed them.

"May I help you?" the woman smiled.

"Yes," Phillip said. "We would like to see Mr. Strauss. Is he here today?"

"Yes," the woman laughed. "Levi is *always* here. If you can wait for just a moment until I finish helping these customers, I'll run back to the sewing room and tell him you are here. What are your names?"

"Phillip and Maria. We met him at his old store a year ago. Thanks. We'll wait."

Maryanne was already deeply into examining the merchandise in the store. She had taken Maria by the hand, and the two of them were happily nosing through the bins and cupboards and going up and down the aisles.

After her last customer, the woman at the register turned to Phillip and smiled. She walked to the back of the store and disappeared through a door there. In a few minutes she returned.

"Levi will be right out. He said to make sure you don't leave."

"Thank you very much," Phillip said, wondering if Levi Strauss would remember them. He looked over to where his mother and Maria were, and saw them both bent over looking at something on the floor in front of them. He could hear their light chatter across the room.

At that moment, the back door opened and Levi Strauss came hurriedly into the store. He looked around, saw Phillip, and walked directly to him.

"Phillip!" he said with his hand extended. "I am so happy to see you again. Is Maria with you?" He grasped Phillip's hand in both of his. The warmth of his welcome was surprising.

"Hi, Mr. Strauss. It's good to see you again. We're really glad to be here." He pointed at Maria and his mother across the room. "Yes, Maria is here. And my mother, too."

Levi Strauss put his arm around Phillip's shoulders. "Phillip, I told you before, please call me Levi. Well, let's go meet them!" They walked over to where Maria and Maryanne were.

At that very moment, Maryanne and Maria were on their

knees looking at some utensils in a large box on the floor. Phillip and Levi Strauss came up behind them.

"Mom," Phillip said. His voice startled them. Maryanne and Maria both hit their heads on the shelf above them as they stood up.

"Ummph", Maryanne said, rubbing her head.

"Mom, I would like you to meet Mr. Levi Strauss. *The* Mr. Levi Strauss. Mr. Strauss, I mean Levi, this is my mother, Maryanne Prescott. And here is Maria."

Maryanne's face showed her surprise and some embarrassment from hitting her head. Levi Strauss extended his hand.

"It is an honor to meet you, Mrs. Prescott. I am very pleased you are here. May I call you Maryanne?"

"Oh, yes, Mr. – Levi. I would like that very much." He turned and held his hand out to Maria. "Hello again, Maria. It is so nice to see you again. It's been a long time."

Maria smiled broadly, her eyes lit brightly.

"Thank you Mr. Strauss, uh, Levi," Maryanne said. I'm sorry. I don't think you know what a pleasure it is to meet *you*." She gestured at the store. "Your store is very impressive. What you have done here is wonderful. We don't have stores like this where we live."

"And that is where?"

"Oh," Maryanne hedged. "It's a small community quite a ways south of San Francisco on the south end of the bay."

"I have heard that the south bay area is nice, although as I understand, fairly rural. Well, what brings you all here, to San Francisco?"

"Actually, *you*, Levi. Phillip and Maria wanted to come and see you, and they wanted me to meet you."

Levi turned to Phillip and Maria. "Well thanks, kids. That was nice of you." He paused. "You know, I have actually thought about you two many times over the past year. And I want to talk to you about it. But let's go back to my office, and on the way I want to show you my sewing and assembly area." He led the way through the store to the back room. They all followed him in. Maria squeezed Phillip's hand briefly and smiled at him. A sparkle of pure pleasure shone from her eyes.

Inside the back room, they were surprised to see four women in aprons sitting and standing around a forty foot long wooden table, which was covered with pieces of dark blue denim material in various stages of cutting. Boxes containing brass buttons and other trim materials were placed in different places along the material on the table. Small wooden mallets and rivets with pounding blocks were also placed strategically by the denim pieces. Off the end of the table sat four large commercial sewing machines.

Levi waved his hand taking in the workshop. "Here is where we build my work coveralls and shirts, and even a few jackets. When we are really busy, I will have as many as ten people working in here." He turned to Maryanne. "And if this keeps up the same pace as it is now, I will have to *triple* the people on the payroll, and possibly even enlarge this area more." He smiled at Maryanne. "What do you think about it, Maryanne?"

"I think it's terrific, Levi. You are obviously very successful. Your store is full of people shopping, and they all look happy. You're employing a lot of people. It seems to be working out very well for you."

"Yes," Levi said. "It seems that way doesn't it? He was thoughtful for a moment. "Let's go to my office so we can talk more comfortably."

They entered a large office, nicely appointed with a large highly polished mahogany desk with a comfortable looking leather chair behind it, and four smaller leather chairs in front of it. Large square windows cut through the wall behind his desk, which let in a beautiful view of the mountains as well as abundant light. The walls had drawings of different patterns of pants hung on them. A calendar sat on his desk, with written instructions and appointments lettered in for different days.

He motioned for them to take a chair, and he held out one each for Maryanne and Maria and then sat in his chair behind the desk. He interlocked his fingers and put his hands on the desk in front of him as he talked. "You know, it's strange. I have thought about this a great deal. I was just barely making it in my old store. The turnaround in my success actually happened the very day that Phillip and Maria visited me. A miner came in while they were in the store and gave me the idea to make pants out of canvas material instead of making tents. My life really changed at that moment."

He smiled at Maryanne. "I almost feel that it was Phillip and Maria's presence here that created the positive environment for this all to happen. After the first samples of overalls I made for that miner, I made some changes in the material to make it more comfortable to wear, and the changes worked well. I can't seem to make enough pants, or fast enough to supply the demand. I almost feel that this was some sort of destiny for me. I genuinely hope that someday many people will be wearing these pants, not just miners. Even people like you, Maryanne. Maybe someday even you – "

His gaze had stopped abruptly and was now focused on the pants Maryanne was wearing. His face paled.

"Maryanne," he said in a voice loaded with emotion. "What are you wearing? Where did you get those pants?"

Maryanne's face turned red. She stammered. "I -, I – "

Levi Strauss was intense. He was standing. "Why, these pants even look like they have been worn a lot." He moved around his desk and looked at them closer, and saw the little red tag. He gasped. "Maryanne! That red tag has my name on it. How can this be?" He moved his head back slightly for better perspective. "How old *are* these pants?"

"Levi," Maryanne said apprehensively. "These pants are over four years old."

"Four years old!" Levi was incredulous. "But how can that be? I've only been making my pants for a year. And look at this pattern you're wearing. I've never seen this before. And this stitching! Incredible! How in the world can anyone stitch like that?

These look like impossible stitches, at least with the machines I use." He went back to his chair and slowly sat down. "Would someone please explain to me what is going on?"

Maryanne looked at her son imploringly. "Phillip, we can't leave Levi hanging like this. You're going to have to figure out some way to tell him about what we are all doing. *All* of it."

"I agree, Mom." He looked his mother. "When we made the decision to continue on this trip after discovering that you were wearing a pair of Levis, I kind of prepared myself for the probability that Levi would notice your pants. And that he sure would be curious about them." He turned to Levi and took a deep breath.

"Levi, this is going to be very hard for you believe. First, the pants my mother is wearing were in fact originally designed by you, and do have your name on them. Where we come from, these pants are called 'Levis', or sometimes 'jeans' generically. When you eventually understand all of what I'm going to tell you, you will be proud to know that your pants are the most famous and popular pants in the entire world. They are *still* known for their durability and comfort. *Everyone* wears them. And not just as work pants, but *fashion* also."

"But I don't understand," Levi interrupted. "You said 'still'. What do you mean 'still'? I've only been making them for a year."

"This is the part that is going to be hard for you, Levi," Phillip said. "My mother's pants were built four years ago in *our* time, but some *150 years in the future* from your time here in 1854."

"What are you saying, Phillip?"

"Levi, we *are* from a town not too far away from here, south of San Francisco, *but* we are also here from a different *time.*"

"What do you mean 'a different time'?"

"I mean, we . . ., we are from the year . . .", he winced as he uttered the words, unh, the year *2011.*"

Levi was wide-eyed, but his voice was low and textured with emotion. "You are telling me that you all are from some time in the future? *Not* this year of 1854?"

"Yes, Levi, that's correct. This visit to see you was because my mother was worried about what we were doing, and kind of demanded to know what this machine we built was all about, and we had to show her. She also had a hard time believing we could actually travel to another time, but we eventually convinced her. She then wanted to meet you, and go through the experience of traveling to a new discovery such as yours." He touched his mother's hand. "Maria and I think she is pretty brave. Anyway, traveling to see the start of famous discoveries and inventions is what Maria and I do. We built this machine to, let's see - I guess "witness" would be a good word – to witness the actual discoveries and see how they happened. We felt that your invention is one of the greatest of these inventions, your *Levis*. So we came here to see how it all came about." Phillip paused, trying to take in Levi's reaction. "You would probably be surprised to know that you are a very famous man in our time."

Everyone sat quietly for a while. Maryanne, sitting between Maria and Phillip, reached out to their hands and held them.

After a long, molasses-laden moment, in which no one spoke, Levi visibly regained composure, and straightened up in his chair.

"Let's get this straight," he said in a tired voice that sounded like gravel. "The reason you and Maria visited me last year – "

"Last week, actually," Maria interjected, "In *our* time."

Levi took that in. "O.k. The reason you visited me was because you wanted to watch the actual moment that I came up with the idea to build pants instead of tents out of my fabric. Is that correct?"

"Yep. That's right, Levi," Maria spoke up. "That, and the fact that we wanted Phillip's mother to meet you personally."

"I'll take that as a compliment," Levi said with a soft smile. "But how did you know where to come, and how did you know about me and my store?"

"Actually, Levi," Phillip said, "Maria did a lot of research on you in encyclopedias and online, and even more research after our first visit."

"What do you mean, 'online'?"

Phillip and Maria exchanged glances. Maria shrugged. "Well," Phillip said with a little hesitancy. "'Online' is a term we use that has to do with a form of communication that was invented in our time. It allows us to do research and find out just about anything and anybody quickly, uh, without, say, uh, going to the library."

"What kind of information did you find on me?" Levi asked.

"Well," Maria said, "I hope I can remember all this. I found out that your real name is Loeb. You were born in Buttenhiem, Bavaria on February 26, 1829. Your father's name was Hirsch, and his second wife Rebecca was your mother. Your father died in 1845 of Tuberculosis. Two years after that, you and your mother and two sisters emigrated to New York. Jonas and Louis, your brothers, were already there and met you at the boat. They had already started a dry-goods business, which they called 'J. Strauss Brother & Company.' You joined them, learning the business, and began using the name 'Levi'. In January of 1853, you officially became an American citizen – Congratulations! – and in March of that same year you arrived in San Francisco on a boat from New York. From the beginning, you never considered panning for gold, but instead planned on selling supplies to the miners. There are a lot of remarkable things you did later, too, but I don't think it would be a good idea to tell you about everything coming up. I can say that you were greatly respected, and that you always insisted on people calling you 'Levi.'"

Levi looked like he was in shock.

Maryanne said, "Maria, that was awesome. I'm impressed."

"So am I," Levi said. "I guess I'll have to accept all this, because there is absolutely no way anyone could have all that information on me. By the way," Levi leaned forward with a smile, "This all sounds like it could have come from the pen of a young writer that is just starting to become noticed in our time by the name of Jules Verne. Have you ever heard of him? Did he become successful?"

Maryanne and Phillip and Maria laughed simultaneously. "Yes," Maryanne said. "Levi, I can tell you without a doubt that Jules Verne did indeed become a famous writer. I used to read his stories to Phillip when he was much younger. He loved them. Jules Verne and H.G. Wells were Phillip's favorite authors."

"H.G. Wells?"

"Oh, I think you will enjoy his writing, Levi," Maryanne said, smiling. "You will be hearing of him soon."

"This is all very surreal," Levi said. "I have many questions. Can we talk about your world, and your time some more?"

They all talked for over an hour. Levi's curiosity was intense. Finally, Maryanne looked at her watch. "I hate to put an end to this," she said. "But the time has passed so quickly, and I am responsible for getting Maria home to her mother. I don't want them to be worried." She paused thoughtfully. "Levi, I've been thinking while we all have been talking. You have been so kind to us, and this is really a historical event in my mind. I would just like to do something for you that might contribute something important to what you are trying to do."

"That is completely unnecessary, Maryanne", Levi said with a smile. "It has totally been my pleasure, *and* complete surprise I might add."

"No Levi," Maryanne said quietly. "I have to do this. And I *want* to do it. Maryanne was beaming. "Levi, do you ever do any trades?"

Levi seemed somewhat surprised. "Well, of course we are always involved in some type of trading in this country. Sometimes I trade out clothing and supplies to local farmers in exchange for food and other services from their farming life. But what did you have in mind?"

"Levi, I saw a beautiful gingham dress in your store that I would just love to have. Would you consider trading that dress for these Levi pants I am wearing?"

"Of course I would!" Levi said excitedly. "But, Maryanne, I would be very happy to just give you the dress."

"Then it's a deal?"

Levi laughed. "It's a deal." He stood and walked to the door, opened it and called out.

"Annabelle, could you come here a moment please?"

One of the ladies that worked in the store entered, smiling. "Yes, Levi. How can I help?"

"Annabelle, this is Maryanne and her son Phillip, and his friend Maria. They are good friends of mine. Maryanne saw a gingham dress in the store she would like to have. Could you please help her find the one she likes in the right size and color, and fit her now? She would like to wear it home."

"It is indeed a pleasure to meet you all", Annabelle said with a gracious smile. "I would love to help you, Maryanne." She gestured to the showroom. "Would you like to come with me Maryanne? Let's go find that dress."

"Wonderful!", Maryanne said, smiling at Levi. The two women disappeared into the showroom.

Levi and the two children talked non stop until a half an hour later when the door opened, and Maryanne stepped through wearing her new dress. She was smiling ear to ear. She pirouetted, did a mock bow, and turned to them. "How do you like it?"

"It's wonderful, Mrs. Prescott!" Maria exclaimed.

"Terrific, Mom. It looks great!"

Maryanne walked up to Levi and handed him her folded Levis. "And this is for you, Levi. I hope it will help you."

"Thank you so much Maryanne. This means a lot to me."

Levi stood up. "I will be forever grateful to you all. This event has changed my life. Is there *anything* at all I can do for any of you?"

"We liked it too, Levi," Maria said.

"Levi," Maryanne said, grasping his hand in both of hers, "I am *so* honored to have personally met you, Levi. I will never forget this. Thank you so much. I wish you the best in happiness and success. And who knows? Maybe we will meet again someday. I know I would like that."

"I would consider that an honor, Maryanne."

Phillip snapped his finger. "Levi," he said. "There may be something you can do if you would like."

"Anything, Phillip. What can I do?"

Phillip walked around Levi's desk and leaned over to whisper quietly in his ear. Levi's eyes lit up and sparkled. "Consider it done, and with pleasure! *But*," he said with a touch of childlike excitement in his voice. "In exchange for this favor, I am asking that you will let me see your time craft before you go. Is that a possibility? I promise you no one will ever know."

Phillip and Maria and Maryanne all looked at each other. A huge smile broke on each of their faces. "Yes, Levi," Phillip said. "I do believe that can be arranged."

Levi was excited. "Well then, my children," he said. "We have one chore to do before you leave, and before you share with me this wonderful experience."

Levi ushered them to the front door. "Sarah," he called out to the woman at the register. "Would you please lock up tonight? I will see you all in the morning."

"Sure will, Levi," the woman said. "Have a good night."

They began walking back up Sacramento Street. As they came abreast of the grocery and dry-goods store, Levi led them into the door. "Wait right here," he said. He walked over to the counter and they could see him speaking with the man in the apron. He wrote something down. He then turned back and met the three of them at the door.

"All right," he said. Let's go outside for a few minutes." They followed him outside again.

"What was that about?" Maria whispered to Phillip off to the side.

"I'll tell you about it later."

They stood outside and talked briefly about the growth of San Francisco. In about ten minutes, the man in the apron opened the door. He was carrying a small wooden box about twelve inches wide by thirty-six inches long. He handed the box to Levi. It appeared to be heavy.

"Thank you, Joseph," he said to the man. "I'll talk to you

tomorrow." He tucked the box under his arm. "All right," he said. "Which way?"

They stepped off Sacramento Street and headed away from the village and toward the waterfront. After a while, they finally arrived at the shed.

"We're here," Phillip said.

"But I don't see anything, Phillip," Levi said.

"Why don't you set that box down, Levi?" Levi set the box gently on the ground.

"O.k." Phillip said. "Now watch this." He pulled the remote control out of his pants pocket. Holding it out in front of him, he slowly moved the lever slightly away from the hover position. As he did so, a faint image of the Discovery Machine began to appear before them. He continued moving the lever until the machine was clearly visible.

Levi's face was like that of a child in delight. "Amazing!" he said.

"Would you like to go aboard, Levi?" Phillip asked.

"Oh, yes! I certainly would!"

Phillip jumped aboard, disappeared, then extended his hand. Levi gasped, but climbed aboard with surprising agility and stood there studying the machine. Phillip pointed to the keyboard and screen. "Here is where we plan where we are going. I'm going to type in the word, 'RETURN.'" Phillip typed it in and the screen responded:

```
Event complete for this trip

     Return is next.
```

Suddenly, a short distance away, voices could be heard approaching. Maria said, "Phillip. Someone's coming. We have to go."

"Come up quickly" he said to Maryanne and Maria. Hand me the box on the way up. Maryanne and Maria hoisted the box up together and climbed aboard. Phillip held out the remote and moved the lever slightly until the DM disappeared from sight.

"Now, everyone be quiet and don't say a word."

Maryanne whispered to Levi, "They can't see us, Levi. We're invisible as long as we stay aboard the machine."

The men were approaching, and they were obviously quite drunk. As they neared the DM, one of them tripped and fell against the machine and promptly bounced off onto his side on the ground.

"Hey, Jim. Now why'd you go and do that?"

"Do what?"

"Push me like that."

"I didn't push you."

"Yes you did."

"No, I didn't."

"You *did* too", the man said, and took a big swing at the other man, but missed and fell on the ground and passed out cold. The other man looked down at him, pushed his shoulder with his foot, and mumbled, "Serves you right." He then stumbled away, leaving his companion lying on his back on the ground.

Phillip said, "He's gone. And I guess we'd better go too." He jumped down. "Levi, I think we have to say goodbye now."

Levi jumped down. He was startled to see the two of them suddenly alone and the DM invisible.

"We're still here, Levi," Maria said. "You just can't see us."

"Amazing!" Levi said.

Maria and Maryanne came over to the edge of the machine and poked their faces out over the edge so Levi could see them. The visual image of two sets of heads and hands coming out of nowhere was a strange apparition for Levi.

"This is quite a sight from down here," he said. "I think it would take me a while to get used to your machine."

Maryanne leaned out a little further from the top of the DM and held her hand out to Levi. "Levi, I don't know if we'll ever see you again. Perhaps we will. But if not, please know that you will be in our thoughts always. Thank you for your hospitality and kindness. There are so many wonderful things ahead for you. I wish we could share them with you."

"Thank you, too," Levi said. "You also have changed my life. I hope I can someday figure out a way to show my appreciation. It was wonderful meeting such a wonderful, adventurous woman as yourself, Maryanne." He spoke to Maria and Phillip. "What you two have done is truly remarkable, but I believe it is more a measure of spirit than technical accomplishment. Make the most out of your lives, children."

He stepped backwards slightly away from the DM and waved. They all sat down in their chairs. Phillip moved back to the controls and pushed the RETURN button. As the DM slowly started its vibrations and increased to speed, the three of them watched as Levi walked over to where the drunken man was lying. He reached down and slowly pulled the man to his feet, putting one of the man's arms around his shoulders. "Let's go, young man. We'll see if we can find you a place to spend the night."

The image of Levi Strauss dimmed, and 1854 San Francisco faded into the past.

Chapter Thirteen: Considerations

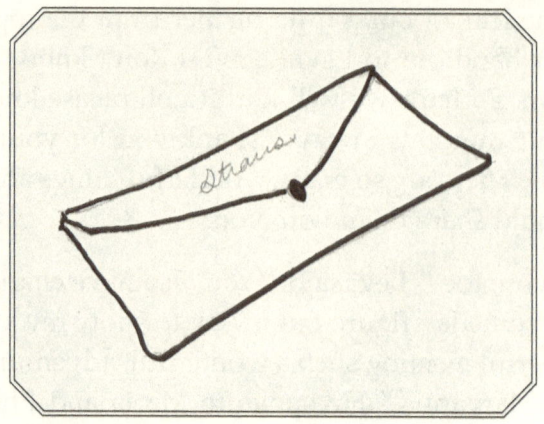

When they arrived back at Phillip's workroom, Maryanne was exhausted. "My gosh, you guys," she managed, "I'm beat. How do you do it?"

"The first time seems to be the hardest, Mom. Are you O.K.?"

"I'm just fine, except for the fact that I can hardly move, and I'm still in complete shock and disbelief over what I have seen and experienced. Look at this dress! Isn't it wonderful? I can hardly wait to wear it at the next country fair." She took a deep breath. "What a trip! I can't believe what we just went through. In fact, I'm not even sure this wasn't just a dream. Listen, you two. Did what we went through really happen? Or did your machine just put us through some type of illusion? Do you think this is what they talk about when they speak of a 'parallel universe?' Did we really travel back in time and meet Levi Strauss, the man who invented jeans?" Maria and Phillip smiled reassuringly. "This is blowing my mind!" She looked at her watch. "Well, we actually made it back, and that's better than I thought would happen when we started out. And it's only 5:30. Amazing." She took a deep breath, sighed, and then turned to Maria. "Maria, honey, what is your status? When is your mother expecting you home?"

Maria was just coming awake. "It's O.K., Mrs. Prescott.

Mom isn't going to be home until about 8:00, and they know I'm over here."

"Well, then why don't you stay and I'll fix the three of us something to eat. But what do you think in the meantime we take a little nap, say for about an hour? I really need to lie down for a little while. Would that be all right with you two?"

"That would be great, Mrs. Prescott. I would like that if it's O.K. with Phillip."

"You bet", Phillip said.

Maryanne crawled down from the DM, followed by Maria. Phillip checked the gauges and dials and the screen, then finally jumped down.

Maryanne headed for the stairs, then stopped. "By the way, I just want you both to know that was fantastic. I don't know how I really feel about this, but thank you for trusting me enough to take me. I promise you I'll figure out someway to handle all this. You two are incredible." She turned and went down the stairs.

Maria and Phillip headed for the couch, and Maria instantly fell to sleep with her head on Phillip's shoulder.

Maryanne's voice was soft as she gently nudged the two children awake. "Hey, adventurers, it's 7:00 and I have some big hamburgers waiting with your names on them. Go wash your hands and splash your face with fresh water and come on down." She walked back down the stairs.

Maria and Phillip stood side by side at the bathroom sink and washed their hands, then shared a clean towel.

"How are you feeling, Maria?" Phillip asked.

"Groggy. And hungry."

"Good. Let's go eat."

Maryanne already had the table set, and the hamburgers were on the plates.

"Ketchup, mayo, mustard, and relish. Anything else? Maryanne asked.

"Do we have any milk, Mom?"

"That sounds good" Maryanne said. She went to the refrigerator and pulled out a carton of milk, and grabbed three bright red glasses from the cupboard. She set them on the table with the carton of milk. "Here you go."

They didn't say much as they ate, and gradually their energy began to return.

"You know," Maryanne said between mouthfuls, "I really couldn't sleep, but I did finally doze off for about fifteen minutes. When I woke up, I believed for a moment that I had imagined all of what we went through, and that I *was* dreaming. The funny thing was that when I realized I *wasn't* dreaming, I felt an enormous surge of relief. I can't explain it. The joy I felt when I realized that I actually had that incredible experience was almost overwhelming to me. I felt my heart beating out of my chest with excitement. But I've got to tell you both, I have never even begun to think I could have thoughts like I had while we were with Levi Strauss. Can you believe it? We actually traveled back in time and met one of the most influential inventors in the world. He is a genuine entrepreneur and we know him by his first name. It is *impossible* for me to take this experience for granted."

She paused, took another bite, chewed it, and swallowed.

"Then, it came to me that you said you have taken several trips. So maybe this isn't so mind-blowing to you as it is to me. I'm a lot better about all of this now, but I still am almost afraid to ask about where you went on your other trips."

Maria and Phillip looked her but didn't reply.

"Look, you guys," she said laughing, "I said I'm *almost* afraid to ask. That was just a figure of speech. That doesn't mean I'm *not* going to ask. Come on. Tell me where else you went. Surely you know by now I can take anything."

"The first trip we took," Phillip said, with a cautious sideways glance to Maria, "was to the year 1943 to see when that strange substance Silly Putty was invented and why." Phillip noted the strange look on his mother's face. "Yup, Silly Putty. We were curious, and that was our first trip, and the best we could come up with at the moment. The next two trips we took were not to times as modern as early San Francisco. We went back to prehistoric time and observed how the wheel was discovered – "

"Or at least *one* version of how it was discovered" Maria smiled.

"- and then we traveled again to see how fire was discovered. Both of these trips were to very primitive times and places on earth."

"There were no problems?" Maryanne asked.

"Not really," Phillip said. He looked at Maria. "We did accidentally leave a thermos when we visited a pre-historic man site, and we're still wondering what those people made of it. Also, we were chased to our machine by a group of people, but that was before we improved the DM controls."

"You were chased?" Alarm was written on Maryanne's face.

"It's all right, Mrs. Prescott," Maria said. "It was a little scary, but we were learning. We won't let ourselves be put in that type of situation again."

"That makes me more than a little queasy, you know." Maryanne rubbed her neck thoughtfully. "Wait a minute. She looked at Phillip. "Is that when you cut your face?"

Phillip nodded.

Maryanne thought about that and frowned. "If anything ever happened to either of you, I just don't know what I would do." She locked her fingers together and rested her chin against them momentarily. "Which brings us back to the dilemma before us. I have enormous responsibility here. What I am going to do with the knowledge I have about what you two are doing? There are many people who would consider my participation in this adventure totally irresponsible and dangerous. Your dad may just be one of those people, and he may be justified. And Maria, what would your mother think of all this? I *do* have to do a lot of thinking about this."

"Mom," Phillip said. "The DM is safe. And we are always very careful. And besides, it couldn't be anymore dangerous than crossing a street at a busy intersection. I mean, we can't just avoid things in life because they may have a degree of danger to them. If that was the case, we might as well board ourselves up in a room somewhere and have food shoved in under the door. *Everything* in life has danger in it. *Life* is dangerous."

Maryanne studied her son closely. "How did you suddenly get so wise so fast, Phillip? You argue a good point. I just want you to realize that it isn't just *you* that is involved in these adventures. You have Maria's life as your responsibility. Do you comprehend that she is blindly trusting you? Phillip, I know you feel that responsibility, because I watch how you look out for her. You two are bound at the hip. I have never seen such a strong and healthy friendship before, and I love you both for it."

She paused and looked out the kitchen window at the trees in the backyard swaying in the soft breeze. "Maybe it's this. I remember that when I was your age I felt I was invincible and indestructible. I had no fear of injury, *or* death. And that is just the way youth thinks. Bad life experiences have not yet tempered you with caution." She paused and smiled at them both affectionately. "On the other hand, one of the complaints I have about being an adult is that many people become so encumbered with fears of what might happen, that it keeps them from enjoying *anything*. Have you ever spent time watching a new baby? *Every* daily experience is new to them. They register pure joy at *everything* they do, and when they can't do something they are angered instantly. They've learned a few *'no's'* and *'don't dos'* from their parents, but *'shouldn't dos'* from their peers and society are not yet recognizable. Those fall under the heading of *interpretations* of rights and wrongs. They have to learn those on their own later, and in the process they may sometimes be knocked around a little. I agree with you, Phillip. Life can be painful."

"Mrs. Prescott," Maria said. "I want you to know that I just don't blindly follow everything Phillip does. I think he depends on me for some common sense, too. Please don't worry. Phillip takes very good care of me, and watches out for me all the time."

"Look, Maria," Maryanne said, "I can't imagine Phillip *ever* having a friend as wonderful as you, and I love you very much." Maryanne reached over and touched Maria's hand.

It was quiet for a moment. Phillip broke the silence. "That reminds me, Mom. There is a surprise for you here."

"A surprise?" Maryanne's eyes lit up. "I love surprises. Where?"

"O.K." Phillip said. "I'll get it. But you're going to have to stay down here for a minute. I'll be right back." He turned to Maria and said loudly enough that his mother could hear, "Maria, keep Mom talking so she won't get suspicious."

They all laughed, and Phillip bounded up the stairs.

Maryanne turned to Maria. "What was *that* all about?" Maria shrugged her shoulders innocently.

In a few minutes, Phillip called out from the top of the stairs. "O.K. Mom. Turn around and face the window, and don't look."

Maryanne looked at Maria with a question mark on her face, then toward the window. "O.K. O.K. I'm not looking."

119

Phillip came slowly down the stairs carrying the box from the grocery store in 1854 San Francisco. He sat it down carefully on the table. "O.K. Mom. You can turn around now."

Maryanne walked back over to the table. "Why, isn't this the box we brought with us from that store in old San Francisco?"

"Yes. It's for you, Mom. It's from Levi."

"What? Levi has given me something? What is it?"

"I guess you'll have to open it and find out for yourself, Mom."

Maryanne touched the box and picked up an old table knife from a nearby drawer. She stuck the knife in the end of the box and pried the end off. As she removed the lid, an envelope fell out onto the floor. "What's this?" She opened it and pulled out a small sepia-colored piece of paper and began reading it.

As Phillip and Maria watched, they saw a tear form in her eye and run down her face.

"What does it say, Mrs. Prescott?"

Maryanne handed her the note. "Please read it, Maria."

Maria read,

To Maryanne Prescott, Adventurer.

Your belief in and support of the dreams of two wonderful and intelligent children will forever inspire me in the pursuit of my own dreams.
Thank you for enriching my life so deeply. I will remember you always.

Levis Strauss, 1854, San Francisco, California

"Aren't you going to open the box, Mom?" Phillip asked.

"Yes," Maryanne said quietly, still emotional from the note. "Phillip, can you help me pull this box apart?"

Phillip carefully pulled the next section of the box apart to reveal an object wrapped in oilcloth. As Maryanne slowly pulled back the cloth, the shiny black and gold-trimmed head of a Singer sewing machine appeared.

"Oh, my gosh," Maryanne exclaimed, "Levi bought me that beautiful Singer sewing machine." She sat down in her chair and stared at the machine. Phillip slowly removed the machine piece by piece until the entire assembly was clear of the box and on the table. He assembled it easily and stood back to look it over.

"I just don't know what to say," Maryanne whispered, almost to herself. She looked up at the kids. "Did you know that when we were standing outside that store in old San Francisco, Levi asked me what my maiden name was? I just flashed on that. Now why do you suppose he did that?"

They were quiet for a while, looking at the sewing machine.

"I've got an idea, Mrs. Prescott," Maria said. "I'll go online and research this machine for you so you'll know more about it."

"And I've got an idea, too," Phillip said. He winked at Maria. "How would you like to visit the man who invented this very machine? And maybe even watch it being invented?"

Maryanne's smile stretched across her face and matched the widening of her eyes.

CHAPTER FOURTEEN: THE RESCUE

Phillip and Maria had met on the sidewalk in front of their school many times before, and were talking excitedly as they moved up the walk toward the steps leading into the school. As they approached the steps, three tenth grade boys who were well known school bullies, moved into their path and stood menacingly in front of them, blocking their way. Maria moved slightly to pass them, but one of the boys moved again to stand in front of her.

"Well." The tallest of the group said, and pushed Maria's forehead haughtily with his pointed finger. He had scrubby punked-out died black hair, with black-died eyebrows also. His ears were pierced with several silver studs of some type, as was his lip. He wore a worn black corduroy jacket with silver emblems hanging from various places, and a light scraggly mustache. His dirty black cotton pants were almost off, and the top back edge of his pants came barely to the top of his cleavage. The other boys were dressed similar, and all had sneering expressions on their faces.

"Well." He said again. "What do we have here?" He sneered with sadistic glee. "Our two school lab rats. Tell me little red-head girl, is this little Phillip wimp bothering you? Just let me know, and I'll take care of him for you."

Maria was hot instantly. "You jerk. Why don't you just go stick your head back in the toilet it came from, and leave us alone."

Phillip immediately tried to push his way between the bully and Maria, and was grabbed from the back by the other two boys. Their books went flying. One pinned his arms behind his back and the other wrapped grubby arms around his neck and began to choke him.

"Let him go!" Maria kicked the boy in front of her hard in the shin.

"Owwww!" The bully reacted by grabbing his shin. "You little wench! Now you are going to find out what the name Bill Bunch is all about!" He pushed Maria hard on the chest and she fell backwards to the sidewalk on her back, screaming.

A crowd of kids had gathered and was surrounding the group at the base of the stairs. Phillip was fighting hard to get loose but the choke hold around his neck was keeping him from breathing, and he couldn't get his arms free.

The bully was now sitting on top of Maria and she was flailing away at his face with her hands, trying to scratch him.

"Nobody's going to help you now!" he shouted. He grabbed her arms and held them out to the side away from her, pinned against the ground. "Now what do you think you are going to do? You going to cry?"

It all happened so fast that it was almost a blur. The two boys holding Phillip screamed out in pain as their knees were kicked out from under them and they fell to the ground, doubled up in agony. In a split second the bully on top of Maria felt himself being ripped backwards by his hair and he hit the ground on his back with a thud. As he hit the ground, a heavy black boot caught him precisely in the groin, and he screamed as the pain surged through his body. He was no sooner on the ground when Moana, the Samoan girl, landed on his chest and pinned him down.

Moana looked down at the bully with a formidable stare and said quietly, "Billy boy, you were always a stupid punk, and you always will be. You like picking on girls, you little coward? Then try picking on me. You want to play the remember the name game? Then remember mine. It's Moana. I am going to be your worst nightmare for the rest of the time you are at this school. If I ever see you within 100 feet of either of these two friends of mine you are going to pay for it dearly. And if you think you can pull that same old crud you always do about having an older brother that will beat me up, well I got news for you. I have a tenth grade brother and a Senior brother, both very big *and mean* football play-ers in this school, who would both be glad to meet you, or your stupid big brother or *anyone* in your family anytime. And if I hear of that happening, I'm going to come after you again, and the next time you won't get off so easy. And if you don't think I'm serious, here's a little parting gift for you."

And with that, the husky Samoan hauled back her arm and smashed him across his face with her fist and broke his nose cleanly. The blood flew across his face and shirt. She got up slowly, looked around at the crowd, and then kicked him sharply in the ribs. He grunted and doubled up in a ball, covering his face. Moana leaned down close to his head and said, "Do we understand each other?"

The bully was blubbering. But with tears streaming down his bloody face, he foolishly said, "You just wait! I'll get you too!"

Moana looked down at him. "I can't believe you said that." And with that, she aimed a carefully directed hard kick at the other side of his ribs, and then reached down and grabbed him by his broken and bloody nose. He screamed in pain again as she gave his nose a twist, and a crunching noise could be heard. "I can keep this up all day, stupid. You better give up while you can still breathe."

"O.K.! O.K.!" he screamed with a muffled voice. "I give up! Just stop hitting me!"

Moana got up slowly, wiping her hands on his shirt and pushing off his chest to stand. "Just remember what I said." She glanced around and saw a teacher running in their direction. She turned to a very shocked Phillip and Maria and with a slight smile said, "C'mon, let's get out of here." Phillip and Maria grabbed up their books and followed Moana breathlessly as the crowd parted in front of them. They moved quickly up the steps and into the building.

CHAPTER FIFTEEN: THE REAL MOANA

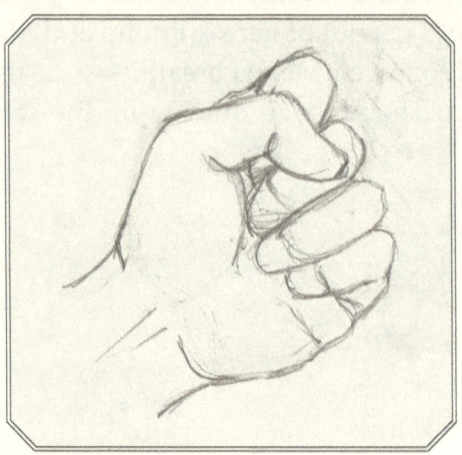

M oana pushed strongly through the front doors of the school to the inside hall, with Maria and Phillip on her heels, looking back over their shoulders to the three bullies still writhing on the ground outside.

"This way," Moana said brusquely, as she turned right up the hall. At the first crossing corridor, she stopped and faced Maria and Phillip, and they stood there gathering their breath.

Maria was holding onto Phillip for support. With wide eyes she said between breaths, "Uh, Moana, *that*," she said pointing outside, "Was, uh, *impressive*. Thank you. I mean, thanks for getting that jerk off me." She looked at Phillip.

"Yeah, Moana. That was *incredible*." He paused, still breathing hard. Moana was looking at them with just a hint of a smile showing at the edges of her mouth. "Moana," Phillip carefully said, "That was a *big* surprise to us."

Maria chimed in impulsively, "We thought you were mad at

us, or possibly waiting for a chance to beat us up, or at the least didn't like us. Why, uh, I mean, what . . . .?"

"It's O.K., guys," Moana smiled. "I'm not mad at you. And I'm not mean. Maybe I just look mean. I'm not any of those things you probably thought. I just don't say much."

Maria was sticking with it. "But how did you know those idiots were giving us a bad time? I mean, you came in from out of nowhere. They didn't know what hit them."

Moana laughed. "Well," she smiled almost apologetically, "I sorta hang around you guys a lot, from a distance you know. I know that you see me now and then."

Phillip's face cracked slightly into a grin. "Yes, we have." His eyes met Maria's.

"Actually," Moana said, looking at each of their faces, "Phillip, I kinda like putting on this "tough" look with a lot of people because I hate bullies so much. This school has a bunch of them and I consider them *targets*. I learned a long time ago that bullies are almost always cowards. They like to pick on people that they can bluff out and terrorize." She laughed. "It really confuses them when a girl gets in their face."

Maria was still digging. "Moana, where did you learn all those moves? You handled those guys so easily."

"My dad. My mom died when I was a kid, and we came over from the islands to California. He bought a house in Saratoga, and he raised me and my two brothers by himself, until he died last year. He was a boxer. Heavyweight. He never lost a fight, but never went professional. He used to tell me that he learned to fight in the streets. He also told me that anything is fair in a fight, especially if someone is trying to hurt you or any of your family or friends. He told me to make sure that when you have someone down, to make sure they don't want to get up and keep fighting, or worse, come back later to try again. So, when Billy boy was down, I thought a hard kick to his groin might get his attention, and then a couple of broken ribs and a broken nose might convince him. I wanted him to be so scared that even the very thought of revenge would be completely out of the question. But, who knows? Some people are really stupid. And he really does act stupid. I kinda hope he tries something like this again. I like messing with him."

"You convinced *me*," Phillip said, smiling with clear respect in his tone.

"Moana," Maria said quietly, "You said your dad died last year? What about you and your brothers? Where are you living? How are you managing?"

Moana put her hands behind her head and stretched briefly, showing little emotion. "Well, when Dad died, my older brother Toa had just turned eighteen, and he legally became an adult in the State of California. My dad left the house in his name."

Maria's eyes widened slightly. "You mean you and your brothers live all alone in your home?"

"Yeah," Moana said, matter-of-factly. "At first, some people from the county snooped around, but we haven't seen or heard from them lately."

They were quiet for a moment. Then Moana said, "Hey guys, believe it or not, I like you two guys. You seem like you really like being together, and that feels good to watch. So I do that. Watch." She paused slightly. "*But,* I gotta tell you, I am very curious about what you two are up to."

Maria looked startled. Phillip gulped.

"Relax, Relax. I'm not going to beat anything out of you." She laughed. "*Come on,* I'm just a big old teddy bear."

At that moment, the late bell rang. Maria looked at Phillip intensely, and he returned the same intense look. "Moana, I think because of how you have protected us, there are a few things that we *might* be able to tell you. Let me and Phillip talk it over. Can we get together sometime next week?"

"Sure", Moana said casually. "That's O.K. with me. Let's go to class."

As they turned away, Maria waved to Moana. "Thanks again, Moana. You were great."

Moana smiled and sauntered away down the hall nonchalantly.

CHAPTER SIXTEEN: A NEW COURSE

It was the following Saturday. Phillip and Maria were preparing for the trip to see the inventor of the Singer sewing machine. Maryanne was out showing property, and Maria had been sitting at Phillip's computer for over an hour. Phillip was fiddling with a new gauge.

"He was a polygamist," Maria said, matter-of-factly.

Phillip was distracted. "What? Who?"

"Isaac Merritt Singer. The inventor of the first commercially successful sewing machine. He had five wives."

"He was married five times?"

"No. I mean yes. No divorces. He had five wives. At one time."

"Five wives. Wow. Wasn't that against the law or something?"

"It might have been a misdemeanor," Maria teased. "Or at least exhausting."

"Funny girl."

"This is pretty interesting stuff," she said, studying the screen. "Apparently there were several people around the world with different but similar machines trying to get them to work right. It appears that Mr. Singer just managed to get his version together before any of the others, and secured the patent. This does say he did have some legal battles over patent rights, and in fact eventually had to pay royalties to Elias Howe, an inventor and machinist from Massachusetts, who had previously patented a working sewing machine. Apparently Mr. Howe's machine had imperfections, and by the time he had worked them out, Singer had already figured out the problems, and secured a patent with a different modified design. But many years later, the courts eventually recognized Howe's design as the original, and awarded Mr. Howe royalties on all other machines until the patent expired in 1867, the same year that Mr. Howe died.

"Where did all this happen?" Phillip asked. "And when?"

"Well, for both Isaac Singer and Elias Howe, it was in Boston, around 1850."

"Then I guess we would be going to Boston, hunh? Mom should love that."

"Do you think she'll want to go again?" Maria asked.

"You bet. I know she'll *want* to go. I also know she's still sifting through her feelings about this whole project." He set the gauge on his desk. "And I don't know what will happen if my dad finds out about this." Phillip sat down close to Maria. "He and Mom are having some problems right now. About his job, I guess. I'm not sure that's all. They haven't been talking very much lately. And I saw Mom alone crying in the kitchen last week."

"I'm sorry, Phillip," Maria said. "I know this is killing you."

"It's o.k." Phillip picked up the gauge again and studied it. "I just want to concentrate on the DM with you." He walked over toward the DM. "By the way, Mom said she would be back around this time. Are you o.k. to go if she wants to?"

"Yup. Of course. As long as I'm home by 6:00 I'll be all right."

"I hope she'll want to go," Phillip said.

The phone rang.

"That sewing machine meant a lot to her," Phillip added. He picked up the phone.

"Hello. Yes? No, she's not here right now. Could I take a message?" He picked up a pen and a notepad. "Mrs. Enright? Yes." He wrote down the number. "O.k. I'll make sure she gets the message. She should be back anytime. Yes. Thank you."

As Phillip headed back over to the DM, they heard the downstairs door open and close.

"Hi you guys!" Maryanne called from downstairs. "I'm home."

"We're up here, Mom. Come on up."

Maryanne climbed the stairs and poked her head inside the door. "O.k. to come in?"

"Come on in, Mom. We're doing some prep for our next trip. How was your presentation?"

"Thanks for asking, Phillip. It went all right. I guess you never know. This is a crazy market. I can't believe how much houses are selling for in this area. It's *unbelievable* what a plain regular three bedroom home in Los Gatos goes for. Even with the economy so bad." She came up behind Maria sitting at the computer and put her hands on her shoulders.

"What are you doing, Maria?"

"I've been researching Issac Singer, Mrs. Prescott. I think you might find this stuff interesting."

"Mom," Phillip interrupted. "You had a call from a Mrs. Enright.

She wants you to call. Her number is there on the desk."

"Thanks, Phillip. This will just take a minute." She picked up the note and dialed the number from Phillip's desk phone. She held the phone impatiently waiting for the ring. "Hello, Mrs. Enright? This is Maryanne Prescott. Yes. Glad to hear your voice too. You have? Which one? You mean the terra cotta three bedroom on Vista Way? That's a great selection. When do you want to go see it? Tomorrow would be fine." Maryanne looked at Maria and winked. "What time is good for you? 11:00 is perfect. Yes. Yes. That's right. Yes, we could probably make that work. I'll talk to the owners. Yes, I don't see any problem with that." Maryanne made the yackety-yak movement with her free hand. "Yes. I agree. Absolutely. Do you want me to pick you up, or would you like to meet there? That's fine. Then I'll meet you there at 11:00 tomorrow morning. See you then." Maryanne set the phone back in its cradle. "You know, if someone would have told me in high school that I would be selling houses when I grew up, I would have never believed them. Oh, well. Now, Maria. You were saying about Issac Singer. . . . ?"

"Well, Mrs. Prescott, take a look at this screen. There is tons of history and material on him. As it turns out, Issac Singer was apparently kind of mean. He was in fact brilliant as a mechanical technician, and a very creative designer. He started out as an apprentice machinist, and although he didn't like what he was doing, he made some decent money for the next nine years traveling around pursuing jobs that utilized his natural ability with mechanics. But it seems his first love was acting, and he quit his machinist work to be an actor. He met and married his first wife and lived for a while in New York. Over time, he was eventually frustrated at not being able to make any money acting, so he was forced to return to his machinist work. He spent time in both careers, and while in Baltimore with a traveling actors group, he met his second wife and married her. By the time he died in 1975 at the age of 63, he had 22 children that were still living, and several more wives. He built inventions for the printing industry, and while doing this came in contact with the early versions of a poorly designed sewing machine that were being built and experimented with. A man by the name of Elias Howe, a brilliant inventor in his own right, had come up with a basic design that had some flaws in it. Other inventors had also devised primitive machines and Singer examined these designs. Singer saw through the flaws in these machines and came up with a design that deviated slightly from Howe's patented design, and made it work. In the process of doing this, Singer did anything he could to promote and develop the machine, many times at the expense of people he worked and partnered with. His partners took the full brunt of Singer's frequent and violent temper tantrums and vocal abuse." Maria looked at Phillip and raised her eyebrow. "Singer ignored written agreements and bulled his way through business relationships. Eventually, Singer brought his machines into international fame, and shipped them around the world. In the end, Howe did win his patent battles in court, and Singer was forced to pay him $15,000 in back royalties. Howe also was able to secure a $5.00 royalty for each machine sold in the United States and a dollar for each sold overseas. This transaction enabled him to bring in $2,000,000, an incredible sum in the late 1850s. Unfortunately, the fight with Singer apparently did him in physically and mentally, and he died in 1867. There was a real difference in personalities between Howe and Singer. They were both credited for the invention of the sewing machine, but their methods of doing business were totally different." Maria stopped and took a breath.

Maryanne had been sitting quietly, listening to what Maria was reading off the screen. She looked disappointed. "Well", she said finally. "It's obvious Mr. Singer was a mechanical and design genius. But it seems that he was also a pretty hostile man. I would really like to think that most inventors were at least a bit more humanitarian. Maybe not. Maybe they weren't. I guess it take all kinds. It does seem that Singer had a big issue with ego." She looked at Phillip and then Maria. "You know, I absolutely love my Singer sewing machine, but I'm not sure I want to spoil my appreciation of it by visiting such an unpleasant man."

Maryanne reflected for a moment, then smiled. "We can

apparently go anywhere we want, and choose events that are enjoyable. Right? Then, why don't we go somewhere else?"

Maria and Phillip exchanged glances.

"That is," Maryanne hastily added, "if you would still like for me to go along."

"Of course we do, Mom. Don't be silly. Where would *you* like to go?"two

"Well," Maryanne said with a sly smile on her face, "I'm glad you asked. It might surprise you to know that I too am capable of doing at least a little research of my own on the net. If you want to know, I've always been curious about lighthouses."

"Lighthouses, Mrs. Prescott?"

"Yes. Lighthouses. I mean, think about it. These are really odd shaped cylindrical buildings with long staircases that lead up to massive lights that can be seen for miles by passing or approaching ships. I've always loved them. I went a step further and found out that the first and most famous lighthouse of all was one of the Seven Wonders of the Ancient World. It was called the Pharos, and it was the great lighthouse of Alexandria. The construction of the Pharos Lighthouse was started around 290 B.C. and it took twenty years to complete. What do you think, guys. Can we go see it?"

Maria was delighted. "That's really exciting, Mrs. Prescott," Maria said. "It sounds great!"

"Consider it done, Mom. I'll get the machine prepped. Why don't you and Maria spend some more time on the computer researching when and where we should go first. Since it took twenty years to complete, why don't we plan making several stops on this trip? Why don't we shoot for when they were planning its location, the beginning of the construction, and when they finished it? Sound good?"

"Oh you guys", Maryanne said, a little misty-eyed. "I still can't

believe you two have put this all together. It's just too fantastic."
She paused for a moment and smiled. "I guess you have figured
out that I have decided to just go for it and experience this to the
hilt. Let's just be real careful. O.k.?"

"You've got it, Mom. Careful's the word."

Maryanne sat down beside Maria at the computer, and Phillip
climbed up on the DM and typed in,

```
       Pharos Lighthouse, Alexandria,
            Start of construction,
                circa 290 B.C.
```

The room filled with the electric excitement of expectation.

CHAPTER SEVENTEEN: THE PHAROS LIGHTHOUSE

It had been two hours since the three of them had decided to change the plans for their next trip to Alexandria. Maryanne and Maria had been at the computer, and Phillip had been working on the Discovery Machine. The door to the workroom and the DM was open, and Phillip was aboard the DM, fine-tuning and adjusting the new modifications he had just added. He stood up, brushed his hands off, and looked the final work over. Satisfied, he jumped down and walked out of the room and over to Maryanne and Maria seated at the computer.

"How's it going?" he asked.

"It's going good" Maryanne replied. "How about you?"

"Good. I'm bringing a small digital camera, just in case we want to catch some records, or document anything amazing that happens. I think it will work out o.k." He looked over their shoulders at the screen. "What have you two come up with as far as our visit dates and times?"

"Well," Maryanne said, "Maria dug up a lot of info on the lighthouse. Really interesting stuff. Especially the info on the designer." She touched Maria on the shoulder. "Maria, why don't you give Phillip a little of what you found out."

"Sure, Mrs. Prescott. The designer's name was Sostrates. Actually, 'Sostrates of Knidos' was his real name. That was the way names were said in those days. I think they generally referred to people by where they were born or what they did for a living, or who their parents were. Like 'William the carpenter', or 'Matthew, son of Peter'. Obviously, when the population increase no longer made that practical, they started placing those second phrases as last names, behind the first name, like 'Mathewson', and 'Johnson', or just taking the profession name itself, like, 'Carpenter'. Anyway, Sostrates had been commissioned to design and build the lighthouse by Ptolemy Soter, who took over power in Egypt after the death of Alexander the Great. He had been Alexander the Great's commander. Well, after helping Alexander the Great complete the new and final city of Alexandria, Ptolemy realized that the two harbors created by the layout of the city brought dangerous navigation problems to the sailors of the time that sailed the area. It appears that the only solution would be to construct some type of large signaling device that would warn sailors of the hazards of the harbor. *So*, Ptolemy decided that the answer was to build a lighthouse."

Maria stopped and sipped some water from her glass. "But let's get back to Sostrates. Both he and Ptolemy were pretty ego-driven. As the construction of the lighthouse continued and developed, it became apparent that it was going to be incredible and unusual in design. Ptolemy wanted to make sure his name was attached to it, thus assigning future credit for the lighthouse to him for all people who would visit or view it in the future. So he directed Sostrates to inscribe the name of Ptolemy permanently and clearly visible on the base of the structure. But it looks like

Sostrates had a little deeper form of planning, not to mention a strong ego of his own as an artist. Get this. What he did was chisel the following inscription directly onto the base of the structure:"

SOSTRATES SON OF DEXIPHANES

OF KNIDOS

ON BEHALF OF ALL MARINERS TO THE

SAVIOR GODS

"What Sostrates did then was very cool. What he did was to have this inscription covered over with plaster, and then he had Ptolemy's name inscribed into this plaster. What was so cool about this was that Sostrates knew the plaster would wear away quickly over the years and this deterioration would ultimately reveal the original inscription." Maria looked at Phillip with a big smile. "Neat, hunh?"

"Way cool," Phillip said.

"Yes," Maryanne said, "And that's what happened. After Ptolemy's death, the full visible credit for the structure became visible under Sostrate's name, and it stayed that way until the lighthouse collapsed from earthquake damage in 1326." Maryanne thought about that for a moment. "I think it's interesting that artists and designers of this level of competency seem to be more concerned about *immortality*, and being famous *forever*, as opposed to the immediate fame and recognition that those in power focused on. In this case, Ptolemy did in fact get credit for this magnificent construction for most of his life, and then Sostrates was credited for it from then on to this day. They both won out."

"Wow," Phillip said. "This must have been a pretty fantastic lighthouse to have people trying so hard to get credit for it. Well, where are we going first?"

"I think we've got it pinned down for the first stop at when Ptolemy was surveying the site," Maria said. That way we can see what the Twin Harbor looked like, and why they were building the lighthouse in the first place. Then, your mother and I thought it would be good to move to construction about halfway through the process, so we can see how they built it. Then we will move to after its completion to see how it looked and how people were enjoying and using it. That sound o.k.?"

"That sounds great." Phillip said. "Are we set to go now?"

"As soon as I can whip up some sandwiches, and maybe Maria can make some hot chocolate." She handed him a piece of paper. "Here are the times and directions from Maria. Why don't you put them in the DM, and we'll go downstairs and get the stuff."

"O.k. Mom. I'll do that. Don't forget to bring some jackets."

Maryanne and Maria walked downstairs, talking excitedly, and Phillip went back into the workroom, climbed aboard the DM, and began entering the directions into the computer.

In a short while, Maryanne and Maria came back up the stairs and into the workroom, carrying the thermos, a small picnic basket, and jackets.

They climbed aboard. Maria stowed the items in the compartment behind the chairs.

"O.k." Phillip said. "I have the information in the computer. We are ready to go! Let's sit down." Phillip and Maria once again sat together in the command chair, and Maryanne sat in the other.

"Everybody set?" Phillip asked.

"Let's do it," Maryanne said excitedly. "Let's go to Alexandria."

Phillip pushed the TRAVEL button, and the machine began to whir.

As things came slowly into focus, they found themselves floating a hundred feet or so above the water, slightly in front of where two extremely large harbors came together. They could see a very large river going off in the distance, and in the other direction they could see a wide channel leading to a very large body of water more inland.

"Wow," Phillip said quietly. "That must be the Nile River. Look at the size of it. I never imagined it to be like this."

"And that water in the distance must be the Mediterranean Sea", Maryanne observed. "So this is Egypt. It's fantastic!"

Phillip pointed. "So they had boat traffic from this point headed that way for Mediterranean Sea business and the other direction Nile River business," Phillip said. "Look at the congestion. I can see why Ptolemy chose this spot to put up the lighthouse."

As they hovered, they could see some four men standing on a point of land directly between the river and the channel.

"See those men?" Phillip pointed. "Let's go over and see what they're up to."

Phillip moved the joystick, and the DM moved slowly over to where the men were standing. As they moved closer, they could see that one of the men was dressed extravagantly in multi-colored robe-like materials, and he was gesturing in broad hand movements while he talked. Another man with long, flowing, black hair, was making notes on some type of pad in his hand. Two other men were just standing there.

"I am guessing that the man in the fancy clothes is Ptolemy," Maryanne said.

"And the man with the long black hair taking notes must be Sostrates," Maria added. "The other two men must work for Ptolemy."

"According to what we found on the net," Maria said, "By the time this was happening, the city of Alexandria was thriving, and known in the world at the time as a port of great wealth and influence. By the way, this city of Alexandria was the last in over 17 cities Alexander the Great built with his name affixed in different locations across the land, most of which vanished. I guess he wanted to make sure his name lasted, also."

"Everybody has an ego, I guess," Phillip said.

"Yup. Anyway, besides needing an efficient and safe way to guide ships through the tricky harbors, Ptoelmy wanted and needed a symbol of prominence and status in the world. So this lighthouse was designed partly with that purpose in mind. To bring fame and stature to the city and its people. And *of course* to Ptolemy himself."

"*Of course*," Maryanne said with a smile.

Ships and boats of all sizes were everywhere in both harbors. It was obvious that this harbor at Alexandria was a major shipping port. And on the ocean, coming in across the horizon, they could see more ships on their way in to the entrance of the harbor. There were magnificent large wooden ships, coming in heavy with two or more masts and sails of all colors, and many of them with deep red sails. There were also small single-masted boats, with colorful sails that extended on long cross beams. The smaller boats were laden with fish, and other commodities from nearby ports, and were manned by one or two men. The larger boats carried large boxes from distant lands, with large pieces of sealed pottery containers. These boats carried crews numbering in the dozens.

Phillip moved the DM toward the Alexandrian port on the Mediterranean side, and into the docking area. He eased to a stop between a large wooden freighter and two small fishing boats. The dock was alive with workers unloading the merchandise, and there was a lot of shouting and activity. In the distance they could see carts both coming and going from the dock area, carrying this merchandise to other places, and eventually to some citizen somewhere, who would choose and purchase an item from a distant civilization, thus perpetuating international trade, and helping it grow.

"Would you like to go see the city?" Phillip asked. "We can stay aboard the DM and just cruise the streets from a safe distance above, if you would like."

"That's a hot idea, Phillip," Maria exclaimed.

"What do you think, Mom?"

"I would love to see Alexandria. Especially in its glory at this time." She smiled with mock seriousness. "I might even want to do some shopping. I've always wanted an original imported Roman vase."

Maria and Phillip looked at her.

"Just kidding," Maryanne said, laughing. "Let's slide on over there, Phillip." Phillip pulled up and back on the joystick and they banked back over toward the city of Alexandria. They came in fifty or sixty feet above the streets, and moved slowly across the town, looking down at the famous city of Alexandria and its people, and how it looked, over 250 years before the birth of Christ.

"Oh!" Maryanne was excited. "Just look at that architecture. Look at how they have designed the roofs with red tile. And they've laid stones on the roadways. And those beautiful arch entranceways to the courtyards and corridors. It's just unbelievably beautiful!"

"Sure is strange," Maria said.

"What is strange?" Phillip asked.

"I mean — ," Maria brushed a strand of hair from her eyes, "Well, we are seeing this ancient city when it was new, and just being built. We generally only see places like this while we are excavating ruins, or in pictorial studies in encyclopedias, with artists' versions of what they *thought* places like this looked like. But *here we are* in the *actual* city of Alexandria. No damage, no make-believe renderings. We're not dealing with examining a cold drawing from some scientist speculating about how it *might have been*. These are *real* people living here doing their everyday things, going about their lives as usual. It's almost like being at home in Los Gatos, watching everyday activities of our city. I think it's just hard for me to realize that we are really here, and not imagining all this."

Below them, a large square came into view. It appeared to be a large open-air market place.

"Look at that!" Maryanne said, pointing. "That must be the central market for the city. Just look at the people below."

The area was about fifty yards wide and long. It had rows of carts loaded with merchandise, and individual areas for vendors. They could see live poultry and other animals tethered and boxed, and they could hear the cries of the animals from where they watched. There were boxes and containers full of produce of all kinds. Other booths displayed cloth and materials of all descriptions. People streamed slowly through the area, picking up items and examining them. There was an on-going audible murmur of conversation between the vendors and the shoppers. There were vendors calling out in loud voices, obviously intent on convincing the shoppers that their wares were the best. They could see customers bickering and negotiating over items with the vendors. Many people were carrying tapestry bags full of purchased merchandise.

"This is a *very busy city*," Maria said.

"You can say that again," Maryanne said. "By the way, did you guys notice that there are not many buildings with much height at all? I don't see anything over two stories. I bet they will be blown away to have a structure near their community that is 400 feet tall, like the lighthouse. Can you imagine? What would they be thinking to climb something that tall and look out over the land? Even just *looking* at something – *anything* - 400 feet tall is bound to be amazing to these people. It would probably be like people in the 1900s seeing the Wright Brothers put an object into the sky for the first time. My bet is that they would be totally amazed."

"Look over there." Maria was pointing to a building that had corridors and separated rooms opening to a field. "Do you suppose that is a school?"

"Could be," Maryanne observed. "Or perhaps a city or community building of some type. Like maybe a city hall."

"This city is probably the most modern city of its time. I can see why it had the fame it did. Alexander the Great must have been driven by more than ego alone. It would have taken enormous insight and planning to put together a city like this. I wonder what kind of man it takes to have the type of thinking necessary to make this happen."

"Well," Maryanne said, "that might be a good subject for some future trip. Alexander the Great wasn't called that without reason. Maybe some time in the future we can visit his time period and find that out."

Phillip thought about that. "Maybe, Mom." He looked around. "Well, shall we head off to the second part of the trip and see what the lighthouse was like under construction?"

"Let's do it." Maria said.

Maryanne said. "Me too, Phillip."

Phillip called up the screen and typed in,

```
Pharos Lighthouse, next segment.
```

They sat back in their chairs as the DM once again began to hum and whir. As they came back into focus, the DM was hovering about thirty feet off the ground in front of the now half-finished structure of the lighthouse.

"Would you look at that!" Maryanne said.

"Wow!" Maria exclaimed.

"That's not at all what I thought it would look like," Phillip said. "I thought it would look more like what our modern type of lighthouses look like. More tubular and cylindrical."

The structure in front of them was far from cylindrical on the outside, and it appeared that the outside was mostly complete. The bottom part was a large square about 80 to 90 feet across, but its core *was* cylindrical, and this core ran up through to the top. The next piece was octagonal and sat in the inside of the bottom square. It was about 90 feet in height. The third and final section was in the form of a circle. It was topped with an eight-sided observation platform. This section was approximately 25 feet in height. The total height of the structure including the base was a little less than 400 feet tall, or about the same size as a 30 to 40 story building.

"Incredible!" Phillip said. He moved the joystick, and they circled the tower slowly from bottom to top, taking in the construction in progress. As they approached the front again, they couldn't help but notice two tall granite obelisks being worked on, some ten feet in diameter and around forty feet tall. The obelisks were covered with scaffolding, and dozens of workers were chiseling away, cutting features into the stone.

"Now, what in the world are those?" Maryanne mused out loud.

"Well", Maria said, "I just happen to have learned about those recently. According to a NOVA special that I just saw on television, these are statues being erected at this moment in time to represent Ptolemy and his wife, Queen Arsinoe. I can hardly wait to see how they turn out."

"Pretty impressive so far," Maryanne said. She was leaning way over in the DM, studying the structure. "You know, designers and architects in those days didn't have any of the elaborate construction equipment we have now. Makes you really appreciate how they could possibly put something of this magnitude together before the time of Christ. Of course, it did take 20 years to complete, but even then, you can see why this was designated as one of the Seven Wonders of the Ancient World. It truly is amazing."

They circled for a few moments longer, then Phillip said, "I'm kind of anxious to see the final product. Shall we move on and see how it looked when finished? Mom? Maria?"

Maryanne and Maria looked at each other and nodded. "Let's go to the last segment, Phillip," Maryanne said.

"O.k. Done." Phillip said. He moved again to the keyboard and typed in:

```
Pharos Lighthouse. Final time segment.
```

The whirring and vibrations stopped and they found themselves hovering slightly above the ground on a dike alongside the entrance to the harbor, some one hundred yards away from the now completed Pharos Lighthouse.

"*Wow!*" Maria said. "*That* is magnificent!"

"Incredible!" Maryanne said.

"Unbelievable!" Phillip said.

"Just look at the statues of Ptolemy and his wife!" Maria exclaimed.

"Well, Maria," Maryanne said, "in what you read, did you find out how it actually worked? How did the lighthouse send light out? There wasn't any electricity, so how could they create a bright beam?"

"They did it with a highly-polished copper mirror at the top, and a lining of mirrors on the interior of the structure all the way to the top, Mrs. Prescott," Maria replied. I believe the mirror was mounted on the top part of the octagon-shaped room, and the light came from a huge fire they kept burning. The mirror reflected the light from the fire at night, and it picked up the light of the sun during the day. What I read about how far the light could be seen was amazing. Reports of this distance were between 35 miles to as much as 300 miles away! Considering the curvature of the earth, the brightness was really amazing."

"Wow," Phillip said. "I almost forgot. We have a digital camera." He moved over to the apparatus he had put together that morning, pulled out the camera, and mounted it on a collapsible tripod. After focusing, he began taking pictures.

Maryanne was examining the ground around the tower. "It appears as though they completed access roads to the tower from both of the harbor areas. I think I read online that this became a major tourist attraction, if you can imagine they had tourist attractions in those days."

"Yup, Mrs. Prescott," Maria said. "It was famous enough for images of it to be placed on coins of the period, and to be mentioned in hundreds of written accounts, including a very explicit one by Pliny The Elder."

"This has been really exciting, as usual I might add." Maryanne said. "I forgot in all the excitement that we have sandwiches and hot chocolate. How about some now?"

"Great idea, Mom. I'm so hungry I could eat a horse." Phillip thought about what he just said. "Actually, that's a pretty gross idea. Why do we say stuff like that? Forget I said it. I'm just hungry."

"Me too," Maria laughed.

Maryanne went to the locker and pulled out the thermos and the sandwiches and set them on the chair between them. As they shared the hot chocolate and sandwiches, they took in the incredible sight before them.

"This has been another amazing day with you two," Maryanne said between mouthfuls. "I hope someday we can share this with your father, Phillip."

"Me too, Mom."

They stayed on the spot for another half an hour, and then Phillip pulled the DM up and they circled the tower for a last time.

"Shall we go home?" Phillip asked as they circled.

Maria and Maryanne smiled. "I guess so, Phillip," Maryanne said reluctantly. "I guess it's time to go." Phillip typed in,

        Segment complete. Return home.

They sat back in their chairs exhausted, as the machine once again resumed its whirring and humming. As they lost sight of the tower, it's strong beam was on a bright line to the sea.

As Maryanne closed her eyes, she revisited the scene above the Alexandrian marketplace, and recalled the words of a poem a close friend had once sent her:

> *Pulsing to life*
> *Streets build and crowd*
> *and the air is soon filled with thousands of impatient*
> *conversations heard from a distance as one voice saying*
>
> *'the strength I possess is of us all together,*
> *   I weaken as we leave finding our single paths . . .'*
>
> *The sun has passed its apex now*
> *and dives gracefully for the valley resting spot*
> *between its pet hills*
> *Streets once more echo with single sounds*
> *Fewer, Fewer*
> *and I hear a low conversation between tired friends . . . .*

CHAPTER EIGHTEEN: THE ACCIDENT

They arrived back at Phillip's workroom at 5:00 tired, but flushed with the excitement of their visit to Alexandria.

As the DM wound down, Maryanne looked at her watch. "Vincent said he would be home by 4:40. You know how he is about exact time. He's probably here, wondering where we are." She turned to Phillip and Maria. "Again. That was a terrific adventure. Thank you both so much. Maria, would you like to stay for something to eat? I'm sure Vincent would enjoy having you here."

Maria picked up her thermos and jacket. "Thanks, Mrs. Prescott, but I've got to get on home."

"You're welcome anytime, Maria. I'll walk you to the door." Maryanne and Maria started for the stairs. Maria walked over to Phillip and took his hand. "Thanks, Phillip. Please call me. Soon."

"I will. I promise." They all walked down the stairs.

"Maria," Maryanne said at the door as she gave her a hug, "Thanks for being so cool and taking me with you. I can hardly wait for the next trip."

"You bet, Mrs. Prescott. See you later."

"Bye, Phillip."

Phillip waved as she went out the door.

As the door closed, Maryanne said, "Your dad must be in his workshop. I'll go out and take a look." She walked through the kitchen and out the back porch to the workshop door and called out. She came back to the kitchen. Phillip was drinking a glass of water.

"He's not here. That's strange. He is never late."

"Why don't you check the phone for messages?"

"Good idea." Maryanne walked over to the phone, picked up the receiver, and dialed in, listening. After a few minutes, she suddenly went pale and sat down quickly, intent on what she was hearing on the recording.

Phillip's heart stopped. "What's wrong, Mom?"

Maryanne held up her hand. She was totally focused on the receiver in her ear. A few minutes later, she slowly lowered the receiver and placed it on its pad. She stared at it.

"Mom," Phillip said, now alarmed. "What is it?"

"Phillip," Maryanne said, with a look of fear clearly etched in her eyes. "That message was from your father. Phillip, I – " She stopped.

Phillip sat down at the table with her. "Mom. What happened?"

"Oh, Phillip", Maryanne said. She reached out and took his hand. "Your father said he just lost his job, and he – I don't know what we are going to do."

Phillip wasn't sure what this all meant. "Will we have to move, Mom?"

Maryanne thought about that for a moment. "I don't know,

Phillip. I just don't know." She paused. "Phillip, your father sounded terrible on the phone."

"What do we do now, Mom?"

"Well, I guess there's not much we can do until your father gets home." She looked at her watch. "The recorder timed his call at 3:15, and it's now 5:30. It's not like him to not call and keep me up to date."

"Don't worry, Mom. It'll be o.k."

"I hope so, Phillip. It's just that your dad sounded so awful on the message. I know he's hurting right now. It's a good thing he doesn't drink" she added almost under her breath. She paused for a moment. "His cell. He always has it with him. I'll call his cell." She picked up the phone and dialed. "Hmmn," she said after a moment. The 'non-connect' recording came on. That's strange." Maryanne walked over to the kitchen window and stood there with her hands on the counter, looking out into the back yard.

"Mom, I'm going to go out on the front porch for a while. Just call me if you need me."

"O.k., Phillip." She turned, walked over, and put her arm around him. "Everything will be all right."

Phillip walked through the front door onto the porch and sat on the swing. He felt lethargic. He didn't feel like doing anything. He was confused, and it hurt to see his mother so worried. As he sat there thinking about everything that had happened, he began to get sleepy, and as his head moved slowly back to the chair, he dozed off.

He was awakened by the sound of car doors closing. He glanced at his watch. It was 7:10. When he turned his eyes toward the sound of the doors, he realized with a shock that they belonged to a black and white California Highway Patrol Cruiser parked in front of their house. Two officers were walking up the front steps to the house. An uneasy feeling dug into the pit of his stomach. He slowly came to his feet as the men approached him.

"Hello, son," one of the officers said in a controlled voice as they stopped in front of him. Is your mother home?"

"Yes," Phillip said, the uneasy feeling in his stomach increasing to a sickening sensation. "I'll get her."

He opened the door and started in. "Mom, there's someone – "

Maryanne met him coming out. "I see them, Phillip." Her face was ashen.

"Mrs. Prescott?"

"Yes. What is it?"

"Could we come in?"

"Is this something about my husband?" Maryanne asked with a quivering voice.

"Mrs. Prescott," the officer said gently. "I think we need to talk with you about it inside. Is that all right?"

Maryanne backed up and opened the door for the officers. On the way in she grabbed Phillip's hand and held on to him tightly.

"Mrs. Prescott," the officer said. "It may be a good idea for you both to sit down."

"Oh, God," Maryanne moaned. She sat down on the couch with a death grip on Phillip's hand. "Is he – ?"

"Your husband is alive, Mrs. Prescott," the officer said softly. "His vehicle went off the road on Highway 17 above Los Gatos, and it rolled over several times. He is in critical condition at the Community Hospital in Los Gatos, and we're here to take you there."

Maryanne put her arm around Phillip and sobbed onto his shoulder.

CHAPTER NINETEEN: THE VISITORS

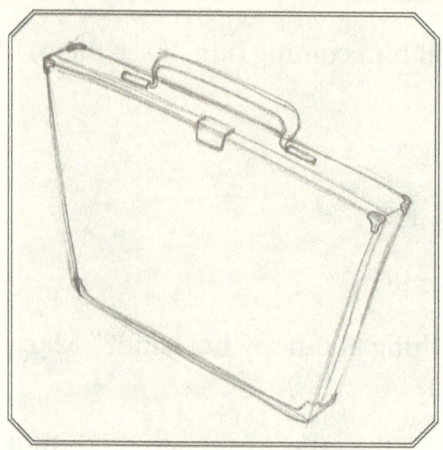

It had been three weeks since Vincent's accident. His condition had been extremely critical. He had remained in a coma for two days before finally emerging to find Maryanne and Phillip sitting by his hospital bed. A serious concussion, two broken ribs, a broken leg, and several bad lacerations requiring multiple stitches kept him in the hospital for two weeks. He was finally released and was now at home recuperating, flat on his back, his leg up in traction in bed in their bedroom.

The decision about their home was tearful, but under the circumstances they had no choice. Maryanne had listed the house for sale on the market, and occasional prospective buyers had already started coming through to look at the property.

It was Sunday morning. Maryanne's brother had loaned her one of his cars, and she was out showing homes. Phillip was standing on the porch looking out at the trees. The sun was playing tricks with the leaves as they turned and swiveled in the light breeze. He was remembering a conversation he and his dad had not very long ago. It seemed like another time. They had been talking about opportunity.

Vincent had turned to Phillip and looked at him quietly for a while. "You know, Phillip", he had begun slowly, "It is all about how we perceive and act on *opportunity*. Opportunities are actually our carrots in life. They dangle around us, temping us with new directions and ideas. Opportunity is really a phenomenon, and a strange one at times, don't you think? Personally, I think it has a personality of its own, and a level of purpose beyond that which we humans can comprehend or assign to it."

Phillip looked perplexed. "What do you mean, Dad?"

"Well", Vincent continued, studying his son's face carefully, "I have often thought that opportunity might after all be a bit *nonchalant*."

"Nonchalant?"

"Yes. It almost has a 'I'm here. Take me or ignore me' presence. To me, opportunity appears to seemingly linger casually by any door, or window, or brain passageway, watching and waiting like a well-dressed vagrant looking for a warm place, waiting for an opening to occur a crack to slip through as if it were a whim of some sort, wisping in on an errant breeze."

"That's pretty heavy, Dad. It even sounds a little poetic."

Vincent laughed at his son's words and shared an intimate glance with Maryanne at the sink with her hands in dishwater. She smiled back.

Phillip noticed. "Sorry, Dad. I didn't mean that I don't appreciate what you are saying. It's really neat to hear you saying things like this to me. I like it." He glanced at his mom, realizing that he and his dad didn't always have a chance to talk like this. He paused, and began again. "I'm a little confused. I've always been curious about how opportunities come about and how things happen, and how sometimes they seem to come from out of nowhere. Sometimes I really search hard to find some way to do something and it just doesn't seem to come for some reason, no matter how hard I work at it. And then sometimes things seem to work when I *stop* trying to make things happen. I can't figure it out."

Vincent nodded his head. "Phillip, things happen for you unexpectedly because you open your mind and subconsciously provide a positive atmosphere for things *to* happen. Also, I suspect that you simply *expect* things to work. Your expectations are high because life experiences have not as yet beat you down and convinced you to think that something can't be done. So you have more things happening." He scratched his head thoughtfully. "I think that sometimes we work so hard trying to force things into the way we want them to go, that we simply block the door for new things to enter."

He leaned toward Phillip and looked him directly in the eye. "Phillip, sometimes we need to just *get out of the way and let things happen.*" He watched his son's reaction. "And any success we might have with taking advantage of opportunities all keys on one thing: Opportunity only wants to be noticed, and invited in. If we don't examine every opportunity when it comes up, then we'll never make any progress."

He paused and smiled at Maryanne. "It's sort of like standing on the bank of a fast moving stream, Phillip. Look out to the water and you can see opportunities flowing past in front of you. You can stand there and watch them go by without examining them, and the odds are they will never come by again, and you'll never know about what might have happened. Or you can reach out and pick them out and examine them closely to see what *can* happen. If they don't work for you, you can always let them go, but if you *don't* look at them they are probably lost to you forever. And remember," he smiled warmly, "It sure doesn't hurt to *believe,* and to have unrelenting faith that what you are after is real. You have to be passionate and dedicated. If you don't have total belief in what you are doing and have a clear image of whatever ultimate goal you have, you will seldom finish what you have started."

That was then. And now so much had happened. So many things had changed. His dad had almost been killed, and everything in their life had been affected.

Phillip went to the kitchen, and fixed some hot chocolate and poured a cup of coffee for his dad. He took the two cups into the bedroom and sat on a chair by his father's bed. He sipped his hot chocolate while Vincent had his coffee.

They talked about small things, avoiding the obvious. "Phillip," Vincent finally said. "I know this whole situation is tough on you, and it's probably hard for you to understand. Phillip. I'm sorry for what has happened."

"It's o.k., Dad. It'll be all right. You and Mom are the best. I know you'll figure out something."

"Thanks, Phillip." The silence was heavy. "I have to level with you. It's not going to be easy. The car was totaled, and even though the insurance paid for it, we can't afford to get another with what was left. What's worse is that because I had been laid off, we had no medical coverage. The hospital bills are huge. Between you and me, I don't have any idea how we're going to be able to pay that bill off, let alone cover our other regular bills. Your mother is working seven days a week, and because she has just started, we don't really have any commissions coming in. Your mother is a strong woman, Phillip, but I'll tell you, she is frightened. I hate to lay all this on you, but we may have to move. We will be through what little savings we have in a month, and I can't be real hopeful about the possibilities of me getting a new job in this area. This entire Silicon Valley is in difficult economic times and lots of *healthy* people are losing their jobs. Jobs are scarce. Considering my condition and the state of the economy, the job issue is pretty dismal. We'll have to depend upon your mother's income, and as you know, and it hasn't really started yet. Sorry to paint such an unpleasant picture for you, but I feel you should know what we're up against. We will all have to work together to get through this."

Phillip found it difficult to meet his father's eyes. Besides the physical pain he could see there, Phillip sensed a deep emotional agony coming from his father. He looked out the window at the two nesting sparrows on the porch roof. They seemed excited and happy, busy going about their business of preparing for their new family. The sparrows seemed so far away somehow, even though they were just outside.

Even at his age, Phillip felt the weight and worry of growing responsibility. He tried to remember what it was like to feel totally worry free. He wondered how his parents were able to handle all the worries and responsibilities of the adult life he shared with them.

An uncomfortable silence lay like a soft blanket over the two of them, muffling their emotions. Finally, Vincent spoke.

"Phillip, I'm sorry I haven't been able to spend more time with you and your mother lately. There's really no excuse, and I am sorry." Phillip was studying the floor and starting to fidget slightly in his discomfort. "Your mother tells me you are turning into an exceptional young man. She also says you and Maria have a wonderful friendship, and that you share a lot of projects of your own design together, although she hasn't really gone into much detail about what they are. She is very proud of you, and so am I." Vincent reached over with some difficulty and touched Phillip's shoulder. "Sometime maybe, when you have the time, I would love to learn about what you two are doing. Is that a possibility?"

"Yeah, Dad. I would love to show you." Phillip tightened internally. He had mixed feelings about what his father might feel about the Discovery Machine if he were to find out about it, especially in the condition he was in. But inside, he knew he would love to be able to have his father enjoy the adventures the rest of them were sharing. Under the circumstances, the emotions in the room were also heavy, and the feeling of uncertainty hung in the air like wet fog.

"Dad," Phillip said. "Do you mind if I go up into my work-room for a while? There are some things I want to do before Maria comes over here tonight."

"Sure, Phillip." Vincent's eyes were damp. Phillip stopped at the door and looked back at his father. There was a deep huski-ness in Vincent's voice. "Phillip, I promise you I will be a better dad from now on. I love you."

"I love you too, Dad," Phillip said, feeling his father's emo-tions. "You are a *great* dad. Just get well." He went out the door.

The stairs seemed to be a little steeper and harder to climb lately for some reason. Phillip wondered how that could be. He paused at the entrance to his room and looked around, taking in what he saw there. He tried to see all the things he had placed there one by one and had become so accustomed to that he didn't see them anymore. He tried to imagine what it might be like to not live in this room. He had never known any other home. And what if they had to move away to some other part of the country?

A sharp pain gripped at his heart thinking about not being able to be with Maria. He tried to push that thought out of his mind.

He walked slowly into his workroom and uncovered the Discovery Machine. He studied it as if he were seeing it for the first time, thinking about what it meant, and the adventures it had given them. He climbed aboard slowly and sat in his red chair. He looked at the dials and screens before him. They seemed to be beckoning him. He could almost sense an eagerness in the machine to get started, to go somewhere, to have adventures, to do *anything* except sit, covered by a blanket in a dark workroom, cold and lifeless like a sculpture.

The reality of the situation was eating at Phillip's heart. Maria and Phillip still spent their time together at school, and spent a lot of time talking about the situation, but they had almost avoided topics centered around the Discovery Machine, and in fact, hadn't taken the DM out since Vincent's accident.

Priorities had shifted. It almost brought guilt feelings to remember the joy of being on one of their trips. At the very least the memories of it brought a feeling something like frivolity, or even carelessness. The memories of the feelings they had shared and the excitement they had felt on their discoveries seemed so remote now, and so unreal. It almost seemed as if they had happened in some other lifetime. Phillip realized, with a feeling edged by sadness, that freedom can be a luxury, and that the luxury of traveling on the DM had a purchase price that he could not at this time afford. He wondered if this was actually what adults were always referring to as 'growing up.' One side of his mind wanted to resist this transition, but another side recognized the inherent force that seemed to drive him toward accepting the lessons that seemed to spill out before him.

Maria had called the force 'subliminal,' and said she didn't think it was possible to avoid the painful things yet to happen in life. "I think we have to learn to roll with them," she had said one day at school. He thought about the word 'subliminal' a lot after that.

As he sat thinking about all this, he once again became drowsy, and soon in the comfort of his red chair, he drifted off to sleep.

He was awakened by Maryanne's voice calling to him from the top of the stairs.

"Phillip. Are you in there? May I come in?"

"Mom. He woke with a start. "Uhh, sure, Mom. Come on in." He rubbed his eyes.

Maryanne came and leaned against the DM. "Hi, Phillip," she said. "How's it going, Honey?"

"Hi, Mom. I'm o.k. How did it go today?"

"Not too bad. I managed to get a new listing, and I believe I'm going to get an offer on a home tomorrow."

"Great!" Phillip said.

Maryanne stood quietly at the edge of the DM. She felt her son's anguish about not traveling in the DM, and knew he was worried. She climbed up on the machine and sat down in the chair next to him. She touched Phillip's wrist. "It will all be O.K. somehow, Phillip. I promise you. Come on. Let's go downstairs. Guess who's here to see you."

"Maria is here?" Phillip's eyes brightened.

"In the flesh." Maryanne smiled.

They jumped down and headed down the stairs.

Maria was waiting in the kitchen. Her smile was wide and genuine. "Hi, Phillip."

"Hi, Maria." Phillip was surprised at how glad he was to see her. He walked over to her side and shyly touched her hand. Maria stood on her tiptoes and kissed him lightly on the cheek. She whispered in his ear softly, "I've missed you, Phillip."

Maryanne turned away to the sink, as a tear formed in her eye. The affection between Phillip and Maria was sweet and untainted. It touched her heart. She opened the refrigerator. "Hey" she said. Her voice was hoarse from the emotion. "Would you two like some ice cream?"

"You bet, Mrs. Prescott," Maria said. "That would be great."

"Well, just sit down and I'll get us some bowls." She pulled out two boxes of ice cream and set them on the table, then brought three bowls and spoons over. "Help yourselves."

As Phillip and Maria dug into the ice cream, she said, "I've already fed your father, Phillip. I guess this would be a good time to talk a little. Is that o.k.?"

"Sure, Mom. Go ahead."

"Well, I know you've both missed being able to go out on the DM. I really am sorry about that. I know personally how important it is to you, because I've been there with you. It's wonderful.

Thank you both for being so understanding about everything we're going through here. I wish it could be some other way right now, but it just isn't. We're trying do everything we can, and maybe – "

The doorbell rang.

"Now, who could that be? It's past 7:30."

Two men in dark suits were standing at the door when she opened it.

"Yes?"

"Yes, ma'mm," one of the men politely said. "Would your name be Maryanne Thomas?"

"Well, yes and no", Maryanne replied slowly. My name is Maryanne Prescott, but my maiden name was in fact Maryanne Thomas. But how could you know that, and what is this all about?"

"Mrs. Prescott, we've been trying to find you for several weeks now. We are attorneys for a large corporation, and it appears that you have been named as a beneficiary to an estate we represent. Could we come in and explain this to you?"

Maryanne was taken back and startled. "I really don't know what you are talking about" she stammered. "I - , uh, do you have some identification?" Maryanne was nervous and suspicious.

Both men pulled out their wallets and presented business cards and driver's licenses. Maryanne studied them closely. "This all seems in order, so come in, I guess. But I'll tell you now, I don't think I can handle any more bad news, and if you are asking for money, we have none." She opened the doors and ushered the men in.

"Mrs. Prescott," the taller of the two men said, "I can assure you that what we have come to talk to you about is indeed good news."

As the men approached the kitchen table, Maryanne said,

"this is my son Phillip, and his friend Maria. Could you please introduce yourselves?"

"Yes, of course. My name is John Stillman, and this is Carl Johnson. You probably do not know of the firm we represent. First, we would like to ask if you had a grandmother or great-grandmother who lived in the San Francisco area in the mid 1850s."

Maryanne's eyes widened. "Yes," she said apprehensively. In fact, my great-grandmother, who I was named after, did live in San Francisco during that period. Her name was Maryanne Thomas, and from what little I learned from my family, she was the original Maryanne. She apparently was a very unusual woman, and my parents thought her name would be a good fit for me when I was born."

"Mom," Phillip interrupted. "You never told me about that. You were named after your great-grandmother? And she lived in San Francisco?"

"Yes, Phillip. She was very interesting. We can talk about that later." She turned back to the two men. "Sorry. You were saying?"

The attorneys appeared a little awkward. "Do you mind if we all sit down?"

"Oh, of course. Sorry." Maryanne said. The three of them moved into to the living room. The two men sat slightly apart on the couch, and Maryanne sat in the easy chair in front of them. Phillip and Maria came in and sat together on a small love seat.

"First, Mrs. Prescott, we want to start off by telling you that as a company law firm, we have been a bit perplexed as to how this information got by us and hasn't been addressed long before this time. Our staff has discovered recently an early provision in a will that concerns you that was apparently overlooked by everyone over all these years. In fact, it just seems to have *appeared* in our studying of original historical documents to the estate. It is very unusual to have missed such an important provision, so we took great care to double check the validity. After months of close scrutiny and investigation, the provision and its authenticity has been proven beyond all question to be valid, and by law we are bound to honor the requirements as set forth in the original will. You are involved directly as the sole recipient to this will directive, as the direct descendent of Maryanne Thomas of San Francisco. We have also investigated and verified her involvement in the directive.

"Mr. Stillman," Maryanne said. "I'm a little confused. What is this will you are talking about, and what is the company involved?"

"Mrs. Prescott. This may shock you to find out, but the directive from which your family was named was from the estate of Mr. Levi Strauss, of the Levi Strauss Clothing Company, based in the United States and Japan."

"What!?" Maryanne looked at the wide eyes of Maria and Phillip who were as surprised as her.

"Yes. Not only did we discover the directive, but also have in our possession a sealed envelope addressed to Maryanne Thomas and family, to be opened upon execution of the will directive. This envelope is certified to have come personally from the pen of Mr. Strauss himself. We have it with us, and will give it to you after we transact this business."

"I have no reason to believe this isn't all true, but I will tell you I am totally flabbergasted. What does this mean? What was the will directive?"

"Mrs. Prescott, we don't know what is in that personal envelope we are about to give you from Mr. Strauss, as by law we were not authorized to open it, but we can be very specific about the terms of the directive." Stillman opened his briefcase, pulled out a pair of reading glasses, and put them on. He pulled out a blue legal file, and opened it to the first page. His voice took on an official tone. "In the year 1854, Mr. Levi Strauss personally made arrangements to have seventy-five thousand shares of original stock set aside for Maryanne Thomas's namesake in the future and formally registered that request. That namesake, by our calculations and supportive investigations, is you, Mrs. Prescott."

"Seventy-five thousand shares of Levi Strauss stock!?" Maryanne was turning pale with shock.

Yes, Mrs. Prescott. Seventy-five thousand shares." Stillman leaned forward quickly. "Are you all right, Mrs. Prescott?"

Maryanne slowly regained her composure, but her face was flushed. "Yes", she said, trying to calm down. "I'm all right." She glanced at Maria and Phillip who appeared to be frozen in place with permanently widened eyes. "Assuming that this is not just some really abstract nightmare, just what", she said, slowly gasping for breath, "does this all mean?"

"Well", said Stillman, peering over his lenses at Maryanne with a concerned look, "We haven't finished calculating the total present value of this provision, but after dozens of stock splits over some hundred and thirty years, and accelerating valuation of the stock to its present sell point of about $3.00 per share, I can tell you that this will leave you and your family suddenly very well off. We are talking about literally millions of dollars."

Maryanne felt like she was going to faint. "This is really on the level. I am *not* dreaming? I mean, this isn't just some mean Candid Camera trick?"

"Mrs. Prescott," John Stillman said, "We know this is difficult to believe. But here is how we will make this real for you." He pulled an envelope out of a small briefcase in his hand. The certified check in this envelope will give you an indication of our commitment to complete our legal obligations. Mr. Strauss' specific directive was that this check should be, as he put it, a "proportionate advance" on earnings and interest accrued. It is made out to you, and can be cashed immediately. Within two weeks, our offices will follow up with a revised statement of your account as to estimated value."

"Mrs. Prescott, this will make you a major stockholder in the Levis Strauss Company. As a major stockholder in the company, you will also be receiving regular dividend statements and future stock options. However, before I give you this payment, and Mr. Strauss' personal letter, we need for you to sign some papers, essentially acknowledging that you have received these envelopes, and that you recognize our commitment to complete the original directives of Mr. Levi Strauss, inventor and founder of Levi Strauss Company."

He handed Maryanne a legal size page of paper and a pen. He pointed to the place for her signature. "Here is where you sign."

Maryanne looked at Phillip and Maria, who were at that moment standing side by side, wide-eyed, and watching Maryanne intensely. Phillip nodded. "Go for it, Mom."

Maryanne looked down at the paper, and spent a few moments reading it. "So, there is no catch? This is essentially a receipt for the check and Levi Strauss' envelope?"

"There is *absolutely* no catch. This is all on the level and legal. And you are right. This is *not* a contract. Also, there is a statement on the page itemizing the logistics of our follow through to assure the payment of designated funds and paper properties to you."

"O.k." Maryanne said, with a nervously resigned tinge in her voice. "I might as well live this out." She looked at the kids and smiled. "Here I go."

She bent over, put one hand on the paper to steady it, and signed. Stillman picked up the paper, examined the signature, tore off a copy for his records, and handed the original back to Maryanne, along with the check envelope and the letter from Levi Strauss. "Congratulations, Mrs. Prescott." He appeared to be relieved. "Here is your starting check, Mr. Strauss' letter, and my personal business card. From this point on, I will be your legal contact with Levi Strauss. Please don't hesitate to call me at any time with any questions or needs, or for cash advances as needed." He dropped the copy into his briefcase and zipped it up. The two attorneys stood.

"Thank you for your courtesy, Mrs. Prescott. We will contact you soon. Congratulations, and good luck."

Maryanne was still flushed as she led them to the door. "Thank you both very much." She closed the door behind them and put both her hands on top of her head and leaned against the door for a moment. Then she turned to Phillip and Maria who were standing in the hallway looking like they were holding their breath.

"Well," she said, amazed at how calm her own voice sounded to her. "Shall we look at Levi's letter and this check from his company?"

"Yes! Yes! Open them, Mom!" Phillip said excitedly. "But let's open the company check and save Levi's letter to the last."

"O.k." Maryanne said. "Done. Here." She handed Levi's letter to Phillip. "Hold on to this." She tore the end off the company envelope and pulled out a folded letter. A smaller envelope was stapled to the back of the letter. "It's a letter from the attorneys. I guess the check is in this small envelope."

"What does the letter from the attorneys say, Mrs. Prescott?"

"All right," Maryanne said. "Here goes". She read quietly for a second. "It's addressed to me, and they even have the address right." She read again. "It essentially confirms what the attorney said when he was here. That the check attached is a starting payment against interest and earnings accrued, and that the company, through their legal department, is committed to fulfilling their obligation to me as the named recipient."

She pulled off the small envelope and opened it. "O.k. Here we go." She averted her eyes and waited until she had removed the check all the way from the envelope.

She looked at the kids. "I'm afraid to look at it."

"Just *do* it, Mom."

"O.k. Here goes." She opened her eyes slowly and let them fall to the check. She gasped and put her hand on the chair back to steady herself. "Phillip. Maria. The amount of this check - ," She was having a difficult time speaking. "The amount of this check is for $1,500,000!"

Maria squealed and jumped into Phillip's arms. The two of them danced around the room and then over to Maryanne and hugged her. "*Look* at this!" She handed the check to Phillip.

"Oh, Mom. This means we don't have to worry about leaving our home any more."

"Phillip, it means *so* much more than that," Maryanne said, an excited tremor in her voice. "This means we won't ever have to worry about much of *anything* any more, including Vincent's medical bills *and* your college education." She turned to Maria. "And Maria, I think *you* can also count on your college education being covered. And more,"she added, smiling inwardly.

Maria could hardly contain herself. She interrupted. "Mrs. Prescott. What about Levi's letter?"

"Yes!" Maryanne said. "Let's read it now. Phillip you have it, so you read it." Phillip opened the envelope, fragile and yellowed with age, and began reading slowly and clearly.

Maryanne,

I have a feeling this letter will find you, and I hope that you and Phillip and Maria are sharing it at this moment. I promised you that I would try to find a way to do something special for you, so I planted a provision in my will for you, knowing that a good attorney someday would eventually discover it.

What you and these two exceptional children have done for me is beyond my ability to verbalize. Dreams, and the intelligent pursuit of them, are as important as any other priority in life. Your encouragement of these dreams is truly inspirational, and it is support of this nature that builds the great works of mankind.

I will always carry with me the concept of your support for their endeavors, and apply this concept to all that I do. I hope someday we will all meet again. I will keep you all in my thoughts forever.

Godspeed.

With great appreciation, I am your friend,

Levi

Levi Strauss San Francisco, California, 1854

They all sat quietly for a few moments, taking in the significance of the letter's words. Maryanne reached down and pulled Maria and Phillip close to her. "Well," she said, her eyes moist with tears, "we have really been on a roller coaster ride, haven't we, guys?"

At that moment, they could hear Vincent calling, and they walked into the bedroom. He was sitting awkwardly in bed, with a concerned look on his face. "*What* is going on?" he asked. "I could hear men talking, and then a lot of commotion. Could someone please tell me what is happening?"

"Dad!" Phillip exclaimed excitedly. "You are *not* going to believe what has happened."

"Try me."

Maryanne moved up and sat on the edge of the bed. "Vincent, we have a lot to tell you. But first, haven't you always talked about your dream of visiting the Hawaiian Islands before they were "civilized?"

"What - ?" He could see the intensity in Maryanne's eyes. "Yes, Maryanne. I have always wondered about what those beautiful people and lands were like before the pirates and traders of the new world invaded them. But what in the world does that have to do with what is happening here?"

"Well," Maryanne said, winking at Phillip and Maria, "hang on to your cast, big boy. Are you *ever* in for a surprise. I just hope you can take it."

"I can take anything you dish out."

"We'll see. Won't we, kids?"

THE AUTHOR

Tom Procter was born in Albuquerque, New Mexico, raised in a small rural farm town in extreme northern California. He grew up with an enormous appreciation and love of nature, and sensitivity to art, music, and writing. Tom taught art, music, journalism, physical education in the California Public School System. After graduate school he directed a small southern California Parks and Recreation District, then went into private business and was National Sales Manager for his own product representation company and an import firm for over 25 years. He is a professional guitarist and vocalist. He was an award-winning paper artist in the mid-'90s, specializing in unique hand-made paper crafted exclusively from indigenous California plants and flora and hopes to re-open this company soon.

Presently Tom is working on two sequels to *The Discovery Machine*, a fiction novel, and a satirical fantasy humor cookbook targeting people who can't cook.

About the Illustrations

Tom Procter went to Thad Smith to see if he would help him find a student from the high school to illustrate *The Discovery Machine*. Thad took interest in the project and ran a contest in his classes. Contest participants read a rough draft the book and submitted their sketches. Thad screened the artwork and Tom eventually selected Joleen and Ariel as the winners to illustrate this book.

Thad Smith, Art Director, Los Gatos High School

 Thad is Director of the Art Department at Los Gatos High School, and has been teaching high school art for eight years: drawing/painting, digital photography, and 3D design. He also works on his own personal work through the name "Thad Smith Studios". Thad is passionate about teaching, and feels at home in the classroom:

"What I really try to get across to the students is that they are all capable. I want them to enjoy the process and not fixate on the end result too much. If they do this, and they do a lot of consistent work, they will invariably improve."

THE ARTISTS

Joleen Guzman, Artist

Joleen lives in Los Gatos, CA. When she isn't busy studying, she paints children's bedroom murals and draws portraits for friends and family.

Her inspiration for *The Discovery Machine* cover illustration came from her own feelings as a child, with the importance of friendship and the undying yearn for adventure. The pen and ink represent everyday simplicity, while the bold colors express the importance of imagination and wonder in life.

Joleen is currently in her second semester attending community college, and plans to transfer to a university next fall, in the hopes of becoming an art teacher.

Ariel Amir Lacey, Artist

Ariel started drawing at an early age and has continued to have an intense focus in fine art, though that now channels itself into her design work.

She began her work in theatre in high school and has since also developed a love for the stage.

She spends most of her time completing designs for her classes and extracurricular projects and continues to do fine art, mainly portraits and figure drawings, in her free time.

Ariel is currently a freshman costume and scenic design student at NYU.

THE NEXT BOOK...

Watch for the next frightening sequel in which Maria and Phillip struggle through an incomprehensible danger, need a desperate rescue from friends in the year 1567, and begin to notice a new and sinister development in the behavior of their time machine.